THE PELICAN SHAKESPEARE

GENERAL EDITOR ALFRED HARBAGE

HAMLET PRINCE OF DENMARK

WILLIAM SHAKESPEARE

HAMLET
PRINCE OF
DENMARK

EDITED BY WILLARD FARNHAM

PENGUIN BOOKS

PENGUIN BOOKS
Published by the Penguin Group
Penguin Books USA Inc.,
375 Hudson Street, New York, New York 10014, U.S.A.
Penguin Books Ltd, 27 Wrights Lane,
London W8 5TZ, England
Penguin Books Australia Ltd, Ringwood, Victoria, Australia
Penguin Books Canada Ltd, 10 Alcorn Avenue,
Toronto, Ontario, Canada M4V 3B2
Penguin Books (N.Z.) Ltd, 182–190 Wairau Road,
Auckland 10, New Zealand

Penguin Books Ltd, Registered Offices:
Harmondsworth, Middlesex, England

First published in *The Pelican Shakespeare* 1957
This revised edition first published 1970

25 27 29 30 28 26

Copyright © Penguin Books, Inc., 1957, 1970
Copyright renewed by Diana Farnham O Hehir, Anthony E. Farnham
and Nicholas H. Farnham, 1985
All rights reserved

Library of Congress catalog card number: 72-95581
ISBN 0 14 071405 7

Printed in the United States of America
Set in Monotype Ehrhardt

CONTENTS

PUBLISHER'S NOTE

Soon after the thirty-eight volumes forming *The Pelican Shakespeare* had been published, they were brought together in *The Complete Pelican Shakespeare*. The editorial revisions and new textual features are explained in detail in the General Editor's Preface to the one-volume edition. They have all been incorporated in the present volume. The following should be mentioned in particular:

The lines are not numbered in arbitrary units. Instead all lines are numbered which contain a word, phrase, or allusion explained in the glossarial notes. In the occasional instances where there is a long stretch of unannotated text, certain lines are numbered in italics to serve the conventional reference purpose.

The intrusive and often inaccurate place-headings inserted by early editors are omitted (as is becoming standard practise), but for the convenience of those who miss them, an indication of locale now appears as first item in the annotation of each scene.

In the interest of both elegance and utility, each speech-prefix is set in a separate line when the speaker's lines are in verse, except when these words form the second half of a pentameter line. Thus the verse form of the speech is kept visually intact, and turned-over lines are avoided. What is printed as verse and what is printed as prose has, in general, the authority of the original texts. Departures from the original texts in this regard have only the authority of editorial tradition and the judgment of the Pelican editors; and, in a few instances, are admittedly arbitrary.

SHAKESPEARE AND
HIS STAGE

William Shakespeare was christened in Holy Trinity Church, Stratford-upon-Avon, April 26, 1564. His birth is traditionally assigned to April 23. He was the eldest of four boys and two girls who survived infancy in the family of John Shakespeare, glover and trader of Henley Street, and his wife Mary Arden, daughter of a small landowner of Wilmcote. In 1568 John was elected Bailiff (equivalent to Mayor) of Stratford, having already filled the minor municipal offices. The town maintained for the sons of the burgesses a free school, taught by a university graduate and offering preparation in Latin sufficient for university entrance; its early registers are lost, but there can be little doubt that Shakespeare received the formal part of his education in this school.

On November 27, 1582, a license was issued for the marriage of William Shakespeare (aged eighteen) and Ann Hathaway (aged twenty-six), and on May 26, 1583, their child Susanna was christened in Holy Trinity Church. The inference that the marriage was forced upon the youth is natural but not inevitable; betrothal was legally binding at the time, and was sometimes regarded as conferring conjugal rights. Two additional children of the marriage, the twins Hamnet and Judith, were christened on February 2, 1585. Meanwhile the prosperity of the elder Shakespeares had declined, and William was impelled to seek a career outside Stratford.

The tradition that he spent some time as a country

teacher is old but unverifiable. Because of the absence of records his early twenties are called the "lost years," and only one thing about them is certain – that at least some of these years were spent in winning a place in the acting profession. He may have begun as a provincial trouper, but by 1592 he was established in London and prominent enough to be attacked. In a pamphlet of that year, *Groats-worth of Wit*, the ailing Robert Greene complained of the neglect which university writers like himself had suffered from actors, one of whom was daring to set up as a playwright:

... an vpstart Crow, beautified with our feathers, that with his *Tygers hart wrapt in a Players hyde*, supposes he is as well able to bombast out a blanke verse as the best of you: and beeing an absolute *Iohannes fac totum*, is in his owne conceit the onely Shake-scene in a countrey.

The pun on his name, and the parody of his line "O tiger's heart wrapped in a woman's hide" (*3 Henry VI*), pointed clearly to Shakespeare. Some of his admirers protested, and Henry Chettle, the editor of Greene's pamphlet, saw fit to apologize:

... I am as sory as if the originall fault had beene my fault, because my selfe haue seene his demeanor no lesse ciuill than he excelent in the qualitie he professes: Besides, diuers of worship haue reported his vprightnes of dealing, which argues his honesty, and his facetious grace in writting, that approoues his Art. (Prefatory epistle, *Kind-Harts Dreame*)

The plague closed the London theatres for many months in 1592–94, denying the actors their livelihood. To this period belong Shakespeare's two narrative poems, *Venus and Adonis* and *The Rape of Lucrece*, both dedicated to the Earl of Southampton. No doubt the poet was rewarded with a gift of money as usual in such cases, but he did no further dedicating and we have no reliable information on whether Southampton, or anyone else, became his regular patron. His sonnets, first mentioned in 1598 and published without his consent in 1609, are intimate without being explicitly autobiographical. They seem to commemorate the poet's friendship with an idealized youth, rivalry with a more favored poet, and love affair with a dark mistress; and his bitterness when the mistress betrays him in conjunction with the friend; but it is difficult to decide precisely what the "story" is, impossible to decide whether it is fictional or true. The true distinction of the sonnets, at least of those not purely conventional, rests in the universality of the thoughts and moods they express, and in their poignancy and beauty.

In 1594 was formed the theatrical company known until 1603 as the Lord Chamberlain's men, thereafter as the King's men. Its original membership included, besides Shakespeare, the beloved clown Will Kempe and the famous actor Richard Burbage. The company acted in various London theatres and even toured the provinces, but it is chiefly associated in our minds with the Globe Theatre built on the south bank of the Thames in 1599. Shakespeare was an actor and joint owner of this company (and its Globe) through the remainder of his creative years. His plays, written at the average rate of two a year, together with Burbage's acting won it its place of leadership among the London companies.

Individual plays began to appear in print, in editions both honest and piratical, and the publishers became increasingly aware of the value of Shakespeare's name on the title pages. As early as 1598 he was hailed as the leading English dramatist in the *Palladis Tamia* of Francis Meres:

As *Plautus* and *Seneca* are accounted the best for Comedy and Tragedy among the Latines, so *Shakespeare* among the English is the most excellent in both kinds for the stage: for Comedy, witnes his *Gentlemen of Verona*, his *Errors*, his *Loue labors lost*, his *Loue labours wonne* [at one time in print but no longer extant, at least under this title], his *Midsummers night dream*, & his *Merchant of Venice*; for Tragedy, his *Richard the 2*, *Richard the 3*, *Henry the 4*, *King Iohn*, *Titus Andronicus*, and his *Romeo and Iuliet*.

The note is valuable both in indicating Shakespeare's pres-
tige and in helping us to establish a chronology. In the
second half of his writing career, history plays gave place
to the great tragedies; and farces and light comedies gave
place to the problem plays and symbolic romances. In
1623, seven years after his death, his former fellow-actors,
John Heminge and Henry Condell, cooperated with a
group of London printers in bringing out his plays in collected form. The volume is generally known as the First
Folio.

Shakespeare had never severed his relations with Stratford. His wife and children may sometimes have shared
his London lodgings, but their home was Stratford. His
son Hamnet was buried there in 1596, and his daughters
Susanna and Judith were married there in 1607 and 1616
respectively. (His father, for whom he had secured a coat
of arms and thus the privilege of writing himself gentleman, died in 1601, his mother in 1608.) His considerable
earnings in London, as actor-sharer, part owner of the
Globe, and playwright, were invested chiefly in Stratford
property. In 1597 he purchased for £60 New Place, one of
the two most imposing residences in the town. A number
of other business transactions, as well as minor episodes in
his career, have left documentary records. By 1611 he was
in a position to retire, and he seems gradually to have
withdrawn from theatrical activity in order to live in
Stratford. In March, 1616, he made a will, leaving token
bequests to Burbage, Heminge, and Condell, but the bulk
of his estate to his family. The most famous feature of the
will, the bequest of the second-best bed to his wife, reveals
nothing about Shakespeare's marriage; the quaintness of
the provision seems commonplace to those familiar with
ancient testaments. Shakespeare died April 23, 1616, and
was buried in the Stratford church where he had been
christened. Within seven years a monument was erected
to his memory on the north wall of the chancel. Its por-
trait bust and the Droeshout engraving on the title page of

the First Folio provide the only likenesses with an established claim to authenticity. The best verbal vignette was written by his rival Ben Jonson, the more impressive for being imbedded in a context mainly critical:

... I loved the man, and doe honour his memory (on this side idolatry) as much as any. Hee was indeed honest, and of an open and free nature: had an excellent Phantsie, brave notions, and gentle expressions.... (*Timber or Discoveries*, ca. 1623–30)

*

The reader of Shakespeare's plays is aided by a general knowledge of the way in which they were staged. The King's men acquired a roofed and artificially lighted theatre only toward the close of Shakespeare's career, and then only for winter use. Nearly all his plays were designed for performance in such structures as the Globe – a three-tiered amphitheatre with a large rectangular platform extending to the center of its yard. The plays were staged by daylight, by large casts brilliantly costumed, but with only a minimum of properties, without scenery, and quite possibly without intermissions. There was a rear stage gallery for action "above," and a curtained rear recess for "discoveries" and other special effects, but by far the major portion of any play was enacted upon the projecting platform, with episode following episode in swift succession, and with shifts of time and place signaled the audience only by the momentary clearing of the stage between the episodes. Information about the identity of the characters and, when necessary, about the time and place of the action was incorporated in the dialogue. No place-headings have been inserted in the present editions; these are apt to obscure the original fluidity of structure, with the emphasis upon action and speech rather than scenic background. (Indications of place are supplied in the footnotes.) The acting, including that of the youthful apprentices to the profession who performed the parts of women, was highly skillful, with a premium placed upon grace of gesture and beauty of diction. The audiences, a cross section of the general public, commonly numbered a thousand, sometimes more than two thousand. Judged by the type of plays they applauded, these audiences were not only large but also perceptive.

THE TEXTS OF THE PLAYS

About half of Shakespeare's plays appeared in print for the first time in the folio volume of 1623. The others had been published individually, usually in quarto volumes, during his lifetime or in the six years following his death. The copy used by the printers of the quartos varied greatly in merit, sometimes representing Shakespeare's true text, sometimes only a debased version of that text. The copy used by the printers of the folio also varied in merit, but was chosen with care. Since it consisted of the best available manuscripts, or the more acceptable quartos (although frequently in editions other than the first), or of quartos corrected by reference to manuscripts, we have good or reasonably good texts of most of the thirty-seven plays.

In the present series, the plays have been newly edited from quarto or folio texts, depending, when a choice offered, upon which is now regarded by bibliographical specialists as the more authoritative. The ideal has been to reproduce the chosen texts with as few alterations as possible, beyond occasional relineation, expansion of abbreviations, and modernization of punctuation and spelling. Emendation is held to a minimum, and such material as has been added, in the way of stage directions and lines supplied by an alternative text, has been enclosed in square brackets.

None of the plays printed in Shakespeare's lifetime were divided into acts and scenes, and the inference is that the author's own manuscripts were not so divided. In the folio collection, some of the plays remained undivided, some were divided into acts, and some were divided into acts and scenes. During the eighteenth century all of the plays were divided into acts and scenes, and in the Cambridge edition of the mid-nineteenth century, from which the influential Globe text derived, this division was more or less regularized and the lines were numbered. Many useful works of reference employ the act–scene–line apparatus thus established.

Since this act–scene division is obviously convenient, but is of very dubious authority so far as Shakespeare's own structural principles are concerned, or the original manner of staging his plays, a problem is presented to modern editors. In the present series the act–scene division is retained marginally, and may be viewed as a reference aid like the line numbering. A star marks the points of division when these points have been determined by a cleared stage indicating a shift of time and place in the action of the play, or when no harm results from the editorial assumption that there is such a shift. However, at those points where the established division is clearly misleading – that is, where continuous action has been split up into separate "scenes" – the star is omitted and the distortion corrected. This mechanical expedient seemed the best means of combining utility and accuracy.

THE GENERAL EDITOR

INTRODUCTION

Vicissitudes of literary taste and temper in the present age have not weakened the hold of *Hamlet* upon viewer and reader, however much they have changed it. Probably they have made it stronger than ever before, stronger even than it was for the last age of men, in the nineteenth century. This is saying much, for men in the nineteenth century helped mightily to make *Hamlet* the most acted and most written-about of Shakespeare's plays. They earnestly accepted its challenge to understanding.

That from which this challenge issues, stamped with a name in words given by Shakespeare to Hamlet himself – "you would pluck out the heart of my mystery" (III, ii, 351–52) – has come to be called the Hamlet mystery by many. Here and there it has been called so with resignation, sometimes hopelessly, but even in its guise of insolubility it can still command critical statement about its being.

It is already plain that the twentieth century will add perception that will matter to the Hamlet tradition in our culture. What it adds will be, like such an addition by any other age, a characteristic enlargement of Shakespeare's dramatic achievement. After a lapse of centuries an extension of perception for a constantly lived-with and experienced work of art like *Hamlet* is an extension of the original creation much to be reckoned with for its revelation of a complex vitality. The new creation comes about not only because the author has conceived form capable of long-continuing growth but also because a late age of posterity, despite the variety of contributions made by former ages, has conceived form into which growth can proceed.

What we in this age seem bent on giving to *Hamlet* is greatly enlarged scope. We are sure enough of ourselves to think of this as meaning a new breadth, and we may hope that it will mean also a new depth. For a long time after Shakespeare there was no generally recognized Hamlet mystery; Hamlet seems to have been for most men a courageous prince who found it understandably hard to take revenge on a shrewd and powerful king. By the nineteenth century the mystery was well established. It was troublesome enough but it could usually be kept within close bounds – that is, within the outlines of Hamlet the man realistically considered as someone who in all essential qualities, however exceptional they might be, could be judged by common sense as a walking and talking inhabitant of the critic's own age. A further limitation came from much thinking that the key to Hamlet's tragedy was probably some one dominant thing such as unstable nervous quality, or shock from his father's death and his mother's hasty remarriage, or melancholy pessimism, or sensitivity unfitting him for the crass burden of his duty to take revenge, or delight in thought unfitting him for crucial action. Such ideas were all, of course, well worth the having, and they shook down into a corpus that will be a lasting part of the Hamlet tradition. But they did not offer enough satisfaction to keep critics from hastening on to other searchings.

Our twentieth-century searchings have become less and less confined, even when they have been within the personal creation that is Hamlet. Hamlet psychology, still very much alive in an age that has produced Freud and Jung, is now not content with merely a homely reading of Hamlet's character by everyday use of heart and mind. The field of Elizabethan psychology has been carefully explored for principles applicable to Hamlet, and thus there has been a fitting of his creation into the history of ideas. With the application of modern psychological theories – especially and most inevitably those having to do with the ancient family triad of father, mother, and child – there has been an expansion of his persona to take account of a dark abysm of the human self from which can come to anyone, as is thought, tensely opposed feelings for both father and mother, and from which, we are to understand, there comes to Hamlet so much emotional conflict with regard to his uncle the King as a substitute father image, married to his mother, that his hate cannot achieve the murder of the King before his bringing, by hesitation, of death to both his mother and himself. Hamlet, indeed, may seem to have been shaped to order for psychoanalysis. In modern psychology an extension of the Hamlet creation, truly meaningful whether one responds to it or not, has been made by the coming together with a startling show of affinity of something in us and something in Shakespeare.

Elizabethan, nineteenth-century, and twentieth-century psychologies often invite us to see within Hamlet some severe seizure of the soul which is close to disease, if not actually disease, and is the more easily thought of in these terms because of the dominant disease imagery running through the play. A Hamlet viewed as thus stricken can be found to have the tragic flaw in an extreme form. Frequently enough an idea has been held that Hamlet shows an exceptionally noble nature and that in this there is, and should be, a classic flaw to make his drama a tragedy. Sometimes the flaw has seemed by no means to be disease-like or wholly undesirable but to take a paradoxical coloring of good from the nobility in which it appears. Yet it has been conceived to be no less an explanatory flaw for all that and necessarily to be delimited, even in the face of mounting disagreement as to what it is exactly.

A part of the present releasing of the Hamlet mystery from its former bounds takes Hamlet the created personality into a realm of criticism where the time-honored idea of the tragic flaw suddenly loses validity. Here there is the thought that imperfection in the hero cannot yield even a part of the meaning in his tragedy by providing some show of justice for what happens to him as an individual. But here at the same time a conception of Hamlet's having nobility of nature remains, and it may go so far as to make him into a type of human perfection. The Hamlet mystery may thus turn into something like a mystery of Hamlet's martyrdom, where whatever makes it mystery tends to be found outside the character of an individual Hamlet in the character of man in general and in the character of the universe which produces the common predicament of man. Man must act, but all action involves him in evil. It is a finding in the content of *Hamlet* that our age has perhaps been qualified to make by its rediscovery of some forgotten powers of evil in human life and by its interpretation of these in recent literature. In such an area of criticism the question is bound to rise, and does rise, whether *Hamlet* is after all a tragedy, whether it is not a drama worthy perhaps to stand with the greatest tragedies but of a kind peculiar to itself. Yet most critics still seem not of a mind to release *Hamlet* from an obligation to show tragic form.

It is remarkable that *Hamlet* should so perplex the mind and at the same time work so little confusion in the heart. It has supremely that which can make us forget our questions when we give ourselves over to it. Probably no other tragic hero of Shakespeare's equals Hamlet in drawing from the observer that most profound pity which is really as much admiration as pity, and is perfectly tragic because there is no condescension in it. It seems impossible not to forgive Hamlet his brutalities to Ophelia, Polonius, or Rosencrantz and Guildenstern, for they are washed out in our feeling if not in our thinking. He should not be made, we believe, to suffer fools gladly, he the superior spirit to add that suffering to his load.

Perhaps more strongly than anything else pity senses the terrible loneliness of Hamlet. The idealism which moves him to a life-and-death struggle with imprisoning evil is so complex, including even a composition of low comedy with high seriousness, that his single companion, the good but all too solemn Horatio, must always be alien to it. The way in which Horatio fails him in the grave-diggers' scene – "'Twere to consider too curiously" (V, i, 193) – is a part of the tragedy, and no minor one. Love desired is always falling away from Hamlet – love in father, in mother, in Ophelia. The poetry that circles about him makes us know that the Prince of Denmark goes through darkness and waste places "most dreadfully attended."

A part of the *Hamlet* that troubles the mind's eye seems to come from Shakespeare's absorption, with sympathies not at all narrow, of a story that had already had a de-velopment of meaning at different depths in different ages. This development had taken place in some rather wide-spread folklore, in a sophisticated literary account of "Amlethus" in the twelfth-century *Historia Danica* of Saxo Grammaticus (printed in 1514), in a very free version of Saxo's account in the fifth volume of the *Histoires Tra-giques* of François de Belleforest (1576), and in an old play about Hamlet on the English stage. Concerning the pre-Shakespearean *Hamlet* we know little. A not very revela-tory passage in Thomas Nashe's epistle to Robert Greene's *Menaphon* contains a reference to "whole Hamlets, I should say handfuls, of tragicall speeches" as being lifted from Seneca, which indicates that a *Hamlet* was on the stage by 1589, the date of *Menaphon*, and that it was a Senecan tragedy. Some even more tantalizing words of Nashe's in the same passage have led many to believe that Thomas Kyd, the author of the Senecan *Spanish Tragedy*, wrote this old *Hamlet*. A performance of it is recorded for 1594 and a glimpse of a part of its action comes in 1596 in Thomas Lodge's *Wits Miserie* with a description of a countenance "pale as the Visard of yᵉ ghost which cried so miserally at yᵉ Theator like an oister wife, *Hamlet*,

revenge." Shakespeare's *Hamlet*, in the present state of our
knowledge, may be dated 1600–1601. Mainly its story follows that in Belleforest. An English translation of Belleforest, *The Hystorie of Hamblet*, was published in 1608 and
seems to have been affected somewhat by Shakespeare's
play. It remains to mention one more Hamlet play, the un-
praiseworthy German piece *Der Bestrafte Brudermord*, the
origin of which is problematic, but which seems to have
derived mainly from an early acting version of Shakespeare's *Hamlet*. The German play was printed as late as
1781 from a manuscript dated 1710.

Some have thought that the Hamlet mystery has been
put forever beyond our understanding by the loss of the
older English *Hamlet*, the so-called *Ur-Hamlet*. Some
have gone so far as to make out that Shakespeare was overwhelmed by matter drawn from the *Ur-Hamlet*, which
turned out to be so unmanageable as he built around it that
the result was incomprehensibility for his joined whole.
That way lies an accusation that *Hamlet* is a failure as a
piece of dramatic art, and the accusation has been made
more than once. Doubtless Shakespeare found the *Ur-
Hamlet* of some avail, and doubtless the *Ur-Hamlet* was a
rude play befitting the dramatic immaturity of its time,
with a quality very different from the mature Shakespearean. But it would seem probable that when he wrote
Hamlet Shakespeare was beyond being overwhelmed by
an old play he wanted to use. He was almost ready to melt
and recast one with complete mastery to make *King Lear*.
As for *Hamlet*'s being a dramatic or literary failure, the
answer of course is that our western culture has forcefully
refused to have it so, and on the contrary has given it esteem of the highest. It is for western man to keep on
asking why, as there seems to be no danger of his ceasing
to do.

As he asks why, it is for western man to realize that he is
posing questions about truth itself, about the glorious but
also terrifying lack of simplicity that truth shows – and

shows in special ways within his own culture – according to a Shakespearean structure of dramatic and poetic images. Here, I would say, is the Hamlet problem of Hamlet problems, one whose recognition lets us know why, after all, there must be many Hamlet problems and various answers to them, yet a gathering together of these into some containing oneness.

The theme of unsimple truth comes early into the Hamlet story. Saxo's Amlethus pretends madness to protect himself until he can get revenge upon the uncle who has killed his father and married his mother. There is no complication of soul-searching and delay in his taking of revenge. He merely bides his time. But there is complication in his procedure of saying things that will make those around him think he does not have the wit to accomplish his revenge. He has not merely that wit but the greater wit to deceive only by being truthful, by turning toward the simple swordsmen who surround him faces of the truth that they do not recognize. He has compulsion never in deepest consequence to destroy truth and he delights in following truth toward a mastery of its complexity. He mingles "craft and candor" to let no word of his "lack truth." There is in him something of primitive riddling, but that is not all. When his uncle's followers think to have sport with Amlethus on the seashore as with a simpleton and bid him look at the meal, meaning the sand, they fully expect that he will take the sand for meal. He not only takes it so; he makes it so in truth. His reply is that it has "been ground small by hoary tempests of the ocean." Here we suddenly know that we are witnessing in fully acceptable form a demonstration of the wide division between the truth of things and the truth of spirit, and the annihilation of this division in the truth of poetry. Such matter as this is largely replaced in Belleforest by a too simple moralizing but not, certainly, in Shakespeare.

In *Hamlet* the theme of unsimple truth is so abundantly restored and so subtly extended that it is everywhere in

the action and the poetry. Hamlet at his first appearance
begins a searching of the complexity of truth by means of
word play and idea play that is carried on throughout the
drama; the craft and candor of his dark rejection of son-
ship to the King and of royal sun-like favor from him, in
the punning words "I am too much in the sun" (I, ii, 67),
are right Hamlet substance and right introduction to much
of the tragedy that comes later. It is by no means only in
words and ideas of the moment that Hamlet stands between truths both to divide and unite them. In the large he
stands thus between whole worlds of truths in our culture:
between the world of an uncivilized heroic past going back
even behind Christianity and that of a civilized present;
between the world of medieval faith and other-worldliness
and that of modern doubt and this-worldliness. In the
same way he stands between the truth of angel-like and
god-like man and that of man the quintessence of dust,
or, in a realm of complete abstraction, between the truth
of love and that of hate. There are, needless to say, count-
less variations in *Hamlet* on the theme of unsimple truth.

It may be said that *Hamlet* is indeed about the pursuit of
revenge but most deeply about the pursuit of truth, and
that the two pursuits come together to give form to the
action of the tragedy. By meeting and testing his father's
ghost Hamlet gains truth that seems adequate. It proves
on second thought to be not enough. By testing the King
with the play within the play he gains truth "more relative
than this." Here is the high point of a rising action. Now
comes a testing by circumstance of truth that Hamlet has
gained with his own testing. He has the chance to kill the
praying King. For some reason (we ourselves never stop
testing to find it) he loses at this moment of opportunity all
truth he has won about revenge as a crying *immediate* need.
He fails to kill the King and thus makes possible the killing
of Polonius, which starts a falling action that carries him to
death – and ironically to attainment of his revenge, a revenge that takes being from tragic defeat, not a revenge in

simple truth such as the revenger seeks. Just before the end, to sharpen the irony, Hamlet uneasily tests his need for revenge against the King all over again, showing inability to make secure in simplicity whatever of lost truth he has regained:

> ... is't not perfect conscience
> To quit him with this arm? And is't not to be damned
> To let this canker of our nature come
> In further evil?

Hamlet dies on the search for truth that all men die on. But his tragedy has a richness of texture all its own, not only within and around the seeker but also within and around what is sought.

University of California   WILLARD FARNHAM
at Berkeley

NOTE ON THE TEXT

Hamlet is preserved in three distinct but related early texts: first, the corrupt and abbreviated acting version in the "bad" quarto of 1603; second, the version "newly imprinted and enlarged to almost as much again as it was, according to the true and perfect coppie" in the "good" quarto of 1604–05 (now usually regarded, but without complete assurance, as printed from Shakespeare's own draft); and third, the version in the 1623 folio (now usually regarded, but again without complete assurance, as printed from the prompt-book of Shakespeare's acting company or from the good quarto altered after reference to such a prompt-book). The present edition is based on the quarto of 1604–05 with a minimum of emendation, but, in view of the manifest faultiness of the quarto printing, with occasional deference to readings in the folio, and even with an eye on the 1603 quarto. Enclosed in square brackets are all additions to the quarto stage directions, as well as additions of whole lines or more of dialogue from the folio. (The longer passages thus added are II, ii, 237–66, 330–54; IV, v, 161–63; V, i, 32–35; V, ii, 68–80.) The texts of the quartos are undivided, and that of the folio almost so since there is no scene division in the first act after I, iii, 1, and no division of any kind after II, ii, 1. It is a common complaint that the editorial act–scene division superimposed on the text in modern times is mechanical and inorganic, and it is supplied in the present edition only for reference purposes. A list of departures from the text of the quarto of 1604–05 is supplied in the Appendix along with a few Supplementary Notes.

HAMLET PRINCE
OF DENMARK

Claudius, King of Denmark
Hamlet, son to the late, and nephew to the present,
   King
Polonius, Lord Chamberlain
Horatio, friend to Hamlet
Laertes, son to Polonius
Voltemand
Cornelius
Rosencrantz
Guildenstern } *courtiers*
Osric
A Gentleman
A Priest
Marcellus }
Bernardo } *officers*
Francisco, a soldier
Reynaldo, servant to Polonius
Players
Two Clowns, gravediggers
Fortinbras, Prince of Norway
A Norwegian Captain
English Ambassadors
Gertrude, Queen of Denmark, mother to Hamlet
Ophelia, daughter to Polonius
Ghost of Hamlet's Father
Lords, Ladies, Officers, Soldiers, Sailors,
   Messengers, Attendants

Scene: *Elsinore*]

HAMLET PRINCE
OF DENMARK

Enter Bernardo and Francisco, two sentinels.

BERNARDO Who's there?

FRANCISCO
Nay, answer me. Stand and unfold yourself.

BERNARDO Long live the king!

FRANCISCO Bernardo?

BERNARDO He.

FRANCISCO
You come most carefully upon your hour.

BERNARDO
'Tis now struck twelve. Get thee to bed, Francisco.

FRANCISCO
For this relief much thanks. 'Tis bitter cold,
And I am sick at heart.

BERNARDO
Have you had quiet guard?

FRANCISCO   Not a mouse stirring.

BERNARDO
Well, good night.
If you do meet Horatio and Marcellus,
The rivals of my watch, bid them make haste.   13

Enter Horatio and Marcellus.

FRANCISCO
I think I hear them. Stand, ho! Who is there?

I, i Elsinore Castle: a sentry-post   13 *rivals* sharers

HORATIO
    Friends to this ground.

15 MARCELLUS   And liegemen to the Dane.

FRANCISCO
    Give you good night.

MARCELLUS   O, farewell, honest soldier.
    Who hath relieved you?

FRANCISCO   Bernardo hath my place.
    Give you good night.   *Exit Francisco.*

MARCELLUS   Holla, Bernardo!

BERNARDO   Say –
    What, is Horatio there?

HORATIO   A piece of him.

BERNARDO
    Welcome, Horatio. Welcome, good Marcellus.

HORATIO
    What, has this thing appeared again to-night?

BERNARDO
    I have seen nothing.

MARCELLUS
    Horatio says 'tis but our fantasy,
    And will not let belief take hold of him
    Touching this dreaded sight twice seen of us.
    Therefore I have entreated him along
    With us to watch the minutes of this night,
    That, if again this apparition come,
29   He may approve our eyes and speak to it.

HORATIO
    Tush, tush, 'twill not appear.

BERNARDO   Sit down awhile,
    And let us once again assail your ears,
    That are so fortified against our story,
    What we two nights have seen.

HORATIO   Well, sit we down,
    And let us hear Bernardo speak of this.

15 *Dane* King of Denmark   29 *approve* confirm

BERNARDO
Last night of all,
When yond same star that's westward from the pole   36
Had made his course t' illume that part of heaven
Where now it burns, Marcellus and myself,
The bell then beating one –
        Enter Ghost.

MARCELLUS
Peace, break thee off. Look where it comes again.

BERNARDO
In the same figure like the king that's dead.

MARCELLUS
Thou art a scholar; speak to it, Horatio.

BERNARDO
Looks 'a not like the king? Mark it, Horatio.

HORATIO
Most like. It harrows me with fear and wonder.

BERNARDO
It would be spoke to.

MARCELLUS   Speak to it, Horatio.

HORATIO
What art thou that usurp'st this time of night
Together with that fair and warlike form
In which the majesty of buried Denmark   48
Did sometimes march? By heaven I charge thee, speak.   49

MARCELLUS
It is offended.

BERNARDO   See, it stalks away.

HORATIO
Stay. Speak, speak. I charge thee, speak.   *Exit Ghost.*

MARCELLUS
'Tis gone and will not answer.

BERNARDO
How now, Horatio? You tremble and look pale.

***

36 *pole* polestar   48 *buried Denmark* the buried King of Denmark   49 *sometimes* formerly

Is not this something more than fantasy?
What think you on't?

HORATIO
Before my God, I might not this believe
Without the sensible and true avouch
Of mine own eyes.

MARCELLUS   Is it not like the king?

HORATIO
As thou art to thyself.
Such was the very armor he had on
61   When he th' ambitious Norway combated.
62   So frowned he once when, in an angry parle,
He smote the sledded Polacks on the ice.
'Tis strange.

MARCELLUS
65   Thus twice before, and jump at this dead hour,
With martial stalk hath he gone by our watch.

HORATIO
In what particular thought to work I know not;
68   But, in the gross and scope of my opinion,
This bodes some strange eruption to our state.

MARCELLUS
Good now, sit down, and tell me he that knows,
Why this same strict and most observant watch
72   So nightly toils the subject of the land,
And why such daily cast of brazen cannon
74   And foreign mart for implements of war,
75   Why such impress of shipwrights, whose sore task
Does not divide the Sunday from the week.
77   What might be toward that this sweaty haste
Doth make the night joint-laborer with the day?
Who is't that can inform me?

HORATIO   That can I.
At least the whisper goes so. Our last king,

---

61 *Norway* King of Norway 62 *parle* parley 65 *jump* just, exactly 68
gross and scope gross scope, general view 72 *toils* makes toil; *subject* subjects 74 *mart* trading 75 *impress* conscription 77 *toward* in preparation

Whose image even but now appeared to us,
Was as you know by Fortinbras of Norway,
Thereto pricked on by a most emulate pride,   83
Dared to the combat; in which our valiant Hamlet
(For so this side of our known world esteemed him)
Did slay this Fortinbras; who, by a sealed compact
Well ratified by law and heraldry,   87
Did forfeit, with his life, all those his lands
Which he stood seized of to the conqueror;   89
Against the which a moiety competent   90
Was gagèd by our king, which had returned   91
To the inheritance of Fortinbras
Had he been vanquisher, as, by the same comart   93
And carriage of the article designed,   94
His fell to Hamlet. Now, sir, young Fortinbras,
Of unimprovèd mettle hot and full,   96
Hath in the skirts of Norway here and there
Sharked up a list of lawless resolutes   98
For food and diet to some enterprise
That hath a stomach in't; which is no other,   100
As it doth well appear unto our state,
But to recover of us by strong hand
And terms compulsatory those foresaid lands
So by his father lost; and this, I take it,
Is the main motive of our preparations,
The source of this our watch, and the chief head   106
Of this posthaste and romage in the land.   107

BERNARDO
I think it be no other but e'en so.
Well may it sort that this portentous figure   109

---

83 *emulate* jealously rivalling   87 *law and heraldry* law of heralds regulating combat   89 *seized* possessed   90 *moiety competent* sufficient portion   91 *gagèd* engaged, staked   93 *comart* joint bargain   94 *carriage* purport   96 *unimprovèd* unused   98 *Sharked* snatched indiscriminately as the shark takes prey; *resolutes* desperadoes   100 *stomach* show of venturesomeness   106 *head* fountainhead, source   107 *romage* intense activity   109 *sort* suit

Comes armèd through our watch so like the king
That was and is the question of these wars.

HORATIO

112   A mote it is to trouble the mind's eye.
In the most high and palmy state of Rome,
A little ere the mightiest Julius fell,
115   The graves stood tenantless and the sheeted dead
Did squeak and gibber in the Roman streets;
117   As stars with trains of fire and dews of blood,
118   Disasters in the sun; and the moist star
Upon whose influence Neptune's empire stands
Was sick almost to doomsday with eclipse.
121   And even the like precurse of feared events,
122   As harbingers preceding still the fates
123   And prologue to the omen coming on,
Have heaven and earth together demonstrated
125   Unto our climatures and countrymen.
        Enter Ghost.
But soft, behold, lo where it comes again!
127   I'll cross it, though it blast me. – Stay, illusion.
        He spreads his arms.
If thou hast any sound or use of voice,
Speak to me.
If there be any good thing to be done
That may to thee do ease and grace to me,
Speak to me.
If thou art privy to thy country's fate,
134   Which happily foreknowing may avoid,
O, speak!
Or if thou hast uphoarded in thy life
Extorted treasure in the womb of earth,
For which, they say, you spirits oft walk in death,

---

112 *mote* speck of dust   115 *sheeted* in shrouds   117 *As* (see Appendix: Supplementary Notes)   118 *Disasters* ominous signs; *moist star* moon   121 *precurse* foreshadowing   122 *harbingers* forerunners; *still* constantly   123 *omen* calamity   125 *climatures* regions   127 *cross it* cross its path   134 *happily* haply, perchance

The cock crows.
Speak of it. Stay and speak. Stop it, Marcellus.

MARCELLUS
Shall I strike at it with my partisan?   140

HORATIO
Do, if it will not stand.

BERNARDO   'Tis here.

HORATIO   'Tis here.

MARCELLUS
'Tis gone.   *[Exit Ghost.]*
We do it wrong, being so majestical,
To offer it the show of violence,
For it is as the air invulnerable,
And our vain blows malicious mockery.

BERNARDO
It was about to speak when the cock crew.

HORATIO
And then it started, like a guilty thing
Upon a fearful summons. I have heard
The cock, that is the trumpet to the morn,
Doth with his lofty and shrill-sounding throat
Awake the god of day, and at his warning,
Whether in sea or fire, in earth or air,
Th' extravagant and erring spirit hies   154
To his confine; and of the truth herein
This present object made probation.   156

MARCELLUS
It faded on the crowing of the cock.
Some say that ever 'gainst that season comes   158
Wherein our Saviour's birth is celebrated,
This bird of dawning singeth all night long,
And then, they say, no spirit dare stir abroad,
The nights are wholesome, then no planets strike,   162
No fairy takes, nor witch hath power to charm.   163

140 *partisan* pike   154 *extravagant* wandering beyond bounds; *erring*
wandering   156 *probation* proof   158 *'gainst* just before   162 *strike* work
evil by influence   163 *takes* bewitches

33

So hallowed and so gracious is that time.

HORATIO

So have I heard and do in part believe it.
But look, the morn in russet mantle clad
Walks o'er the dew of yon high eastward hill.
Break we our watch up, and by my advice
Let us impart what we have seen to-night
Unto young Hamlet, for upon my life
This spirit, dumb to us, will speak to him.
Do you consent we shall acquaint him with it,
As needful in our loves, fitting our duty?

MARCELLUS

Let's do't, I pray, and I this morning know
Where we shall find him most conveniently.   *Exeunt.*

*

I, ii   *Flourish. Enter Claudius, King of Denmark,*
Gertrude the Queen, Councillors, Polonius and his
son Laertes, Hamlet, cum aliis [including Voltemand
and Cornelius].

KING

Though yet of Hamlet our dear brother's death
The memory be green, and that it us befitted
To bear our hearts in grief, and our whole kingdom
To be contracted in one brow of woe,
Yet so far hath discretion fought with nature
That we with wisest sorrow think on him
Together with remembrance of ourselves.
Therefore our sometime sister, now our queen,
9   Th' imperial jointress to this warlike state,
Have we, as 'twere with a defeated joy,
With an auspicious and a dropping eye,
With mirth in funeral and with dirge in marriage,

I, ii Elsinore Castle: a room of state   s.d. *cum aliis* with others   **9** *jointress*
a woman who has a jointure, or joint tenancy of an estate

In equal scale weighing delight and dole,
Taken to wife. Nor have we herein barred   14
Your better wisdoms, which have freely gone
With this affair along. For all, our thanks.
Now follows, that you know, young Fortinbras,
Holding a weak supposal of our worth,
Or thinking by our late dear brother's death
Our state to be disjoint and out of frame,
Colleaguèd with this dream of his advantage,   21
He hath not failed to pester us with message
Importing the surrender of those lands
Lost by his father, with all bands of law,
To our most valiant brother. So much for him.
Now for ourself and for this time of meeting.
Thus much the business is : we have here writ
To Norway, uncle of young Fortinbras –
Who, impotent and bedrid, scarcely hears
Of this his nephew's purpose – to suppress
His further gait herein, in that the levies,   31
The lists, and full proportions are all made   32
Out of his subject ; and we here dispatch
You, good Cornelius, and you, Voltemand,
For bearers of this greeting to old Norway,
Giving to you no further personal power
To business with the king, more than the scope
Of these delated articles allow.   38
Farewell, and let your haste commend your duty.

CORNELIUS, VOLTEMAND
    In that, and all things, will we show our duty.

KING
    We doubt it nothing. Heartily farewell.
                    [Exeunt Voltemand and Cornelius.]
    And now, Laertes, what's the news with you ?
    You told us of some suit. What is't, Laertes ?

14 *barred* excluded   21 *Colleaguèd* united   31 *gait* going   32 *proportions*
amounts of forces and supplies   38 *delated* detailed

35

44   You cannot speak of reason to the Dane
45   And lose your voice. What wouldst thou beg, Laertes.
      That shall not be my offer, not thy asking?
47   The head is not more native to the heart,
48   The hand more instrumental to the mouth,
      Than is the throne of Denmark to thy father.
      What wouldst thou have, Laertes?

LAERTES   My dread lord,
      Your leave and favor to return to France,
      From whence though willingly I came to Denmark
      To show my duty in your coronation,
      Yet now I must confess, that duty done,
      My thoughts and wishes bend again toward France
      And bow them to your gracious leave and pardon.

KING
      Have you your father's leave? What says Polonius?

POLONIUS
      He hath, my lord, wrung from me my slow leave
      By laborsome petition, and at last
      Upon his will I sealed my hard consent.
      I do beseech you give him leave to go.

KING
      Take thy fair hour, Laertes. Time be thine,
      And thy best graces spend it at thy will.
64   But now, my cousin Hamlet, and my son –

HAMLET [aside]
65   A little more than kin, and less than kind!

KING
      How is it that the clouds still hang on you?

HAMLET
67   Not so, my lord. I am too much in the sun.

---

44 *Dane* King of Denmark 45 *lose your voice* speak in vain 47 *native* joined
by nature 48 *instrumental* serviceable 64 *cousin* kinsman more distant
than parent, child, brother, or sister 65 *kin* related as nephew; *kind* kindly
in feeling, as by kind, or nature, a son would be to his father 67 *sun* sun-
shine of the king's undesired favor (with the punning additional meaning of
'place of a son')

QUEEN
   Good Hamlet, cast thy nighted color off,
   And let thine eye look like a friend on Denmark.
   Do not for ever with thy vailèd lids   70
   Seek for thy noble father in the dust.
   Thou know'st 'tis common. All that lives must die,
   Passing through nature to eternity.

HAMLET
   Ay, madam, it is common.

QUEEN   If it be,
   Why seems it so particular with thee?

HAMLET
   Seems, madam? Nay, it is. I know not 'seems.'
   'Tis not alone my inky cloak, good mother,
   Nor customary suits of solemn black,
   Nor windy suspiration of forced breath,
   No, nor the fruitful river in the eye,   80
   Nor the dejected havior of the visage,
   Together with all forms, moods, shapes of grief,
   That can denote me truly. These indeed seem,
   For they are actions that a man might play,
   But I have that within which passeth show –
   These but the trappings and the suits of woe.

KING
   'Tis sweet and commendable in your nature, Hamlet,
   To give these mourning duties to your father,
   But you must know your father lost a father,
   That father lost, lost his, and the survivor bound
   In filial obligation for some term
   To do obsequious sorrow. But to persever   92
   In obstinate condolement is a course
   Of impious stubbornness. 'Tis unmanly grief.
   It shows a will most incorrect to heaven,
   A heart unfortified, a mind impatient,

70 *vailèd* downcast   92 *obsequious* proper to obsequies or funerals; *persever*
persevere (accented on the second syllable, as always in Shakespeare)

An understanding simple and unschooled.
For what we know must be and is as common
As any the most vulgar thing to sense,
100   Why should we in our peevish opposition
Take it to heart? Fie, 'tis a fault to heaven,
A fault against the dead, a fault to nature,
To reason most absurd, whose common theme
Is death of fathers, and who still hath cried,
From the first corse till he that died to-day,
'This must be so.' We pray you throw to earth
This unprevailing woe, and think of us
As of a father, for let the world take note
You are the most immediate to our throne,
And with no less nobility of love
Than that which dearest father bears his son
Do I impart toward you. For your intent
In going back to school in Wittenberg,
114   It is most retrograde to our desire,
And we beseech you, bend you to remain
Here in the cheer and comfort of our eye,
Our chiefest courtier, cousin, and our son.

QUEEN

Let not thy mother lose her prayers, Hamlet.
I pray thee stay with us, go not to Wittenberg.

HAMLET

I shall in all my best obey you, madam.

KING

Why, 'tis a loving and a fair reply.
Be as ourself in Denmark. Madam, come.
This gentle and unforced accord of Hamlet
Sits smiling to my heart, in grace whereof
No jocund health that Denmark drinks to-day
But the great cannon to the clouds shall tell,
127   And the king's rouse the heaven shall bruit again,
Respeaking earthly thunder. Come away.

Flourish. Exeunt all but Hamlet.

114 *retrograde* contrary   127 *rouse* toast drunk in wine; *bruit* echo

HAMLET

O that this too too sullied flesh would melt,   129
Thaw, and resolve itself into a dew,
Or that the Everlasting had not fixed
His canon 'gainst self-slaughter. O God, God,   132
How weary, stale, flat, and unprofitable
Seem to me all the uses of this world!
Fie on't, ah, fie, 'tis an unweeded garden
That grows to seed. Things rank and gross in nature
Possess it merely. That it should come to this,   137
But two months dead, nay, not so much, not two,
So excellent a king, that was to this
Hyperion to a satyr, so loving to my mother   140
That he might not beteem the winds of heaven   141
Visit her face too roughly. Heaven and earth,
Must I remember? Why, she would hang on him
As if increase of appetite had grown
By what it fed on, and yet within a month –
Let me not think on't; frailty, thy name is woman –
A little month, or ere those shoes were old
With which she followed my poor father's body
Like Niobe, all tears, why she, even she –   149
O God, a beast that wants discourse of reason   150
Would have mourned longer – married with my uncle,
My father's brother, but no more like my father
Than I to Hercules. Within a month,
Ere yet the salt of most unrighteous tears
Had left the flushing in her gallèd eyes,   155
She married. O, most wicked speed, to post
With such dexterity to incestuous sheets!

---

129 *sullied* (see Appendix: Supplementary Notes) 132 *canon* law 137 *merely* completely 140 *Hyperion* the sun god 141 *beteem* allow 149 *Niobe* the proud mother who boasted of having more children than Leto and was punished when they were slain by Apollo and Artemis, children of Leto; the grieving Niobe was changed by Zeus into a stone, which continually dropped tears 150 *discourse* logical power or process 155 *gallèd* irritated

It is not nor it cannot come to good.
But break my heart, for I must hold my tongue.
Enter Horatio, Marcellus, and Bernardo.

HORATIO
Hail to your lordship!

HAMLET   I am glad to see you well.
Horatio – or I do forget myself.

HORATIO
The same, my lord, and your poor servant ever.

HAMLET

163 Sir, my good friend, I'll change that name with you.
164 And what make you from Wittenberg, Horatio?
Marcellus?

MARCELLUS My good lord!

HAMLET
I am very glad to see you. *[to Bernardo]* Good even, sir.
But what, in faith, make you from Wittenberg?

HORATIO
A truant disposition, good my lord.

HAMLET
I would not hear your enemy say so,
Nor shall you do my ear that violence
To make it truster of your own report
Against yourself. I know you are no truant.
But what is your affair in Elsinore?
We'll teach you to drink deep ere you depart.

HORATIO
My lord, I came to see your father's funeral.

HAMLET
I prithee do not mock me, fellow student.
I think it was to see my mother's wedding.

HORATIO
Indeed, my lord, it followed hard upon.

HAMLET
Thrift, thrift, Horatio. The funeral baked meats

163 *change* exchange   164 *make* do

Did coldly furnish forth the marriage tables.
Would I had met my dearest foe in heaven   182
Or ever I had seen that day, Horatio!
My father – methinks I see my father.

HORATIO
Where, my lord?

HAMLET   In my mind's eye, Horatio.

HORATIO
I saw him once. 'A was a goodly king.

HAMLET
'A was a man, take him for all in all,
I shall not look upon his like again.

HORATIO
My lord, I think I saw him yesternight.

HAMLET Saw? who?

HORATIO
My lord, the king your father.

HAMLET   The king my father?

HORATIO
Season your admiration for a while   192
With an attent ear till I may deliver
Upon the witness of these gentlemen
This marvel to you.

HAMLET   For God's love let me hear!

HORATIO
Two nights together had these gentlemen,
Marcellus and Bernardo, on their watch
In the dead waste and middle of the night
Been thus encountered. A figure like your father,
Armèd at point exactly, cap-a-pe,   200
Appears before them and with solemn march
Goes slow and stately by them. Thrice he walked
By their oppressed and fear-surprisèd eyes

---

182 *dearest* direst, bitterest 192 *Season your admiration* control your
wonder 200 *at point* completely; *cap-a-pe* from head to foot

204 Within his truncheon's length, whilst they, distilled
Almost to jelly with the act of fear,
Stand dumb and speak not to him. This to me
In dreadful secrecy impart they did,
And I with them the third night kept the watch,
Where, as they had delivered, both in time,
Form of the thing, each word made true and good,
The apparition comes. I knew your father.
These hands are not more like.

HAMLET   But where was this?
MARCELLUS
My lord, upon the platform where we watched.
HAMLET
Did you not speak to it?
HORATIO   My lord, I did,
But answer made it none. Yet once methought
216 It lifted up it head and did address
Itself to motion like as it would speak.
But even then the morning cock crew loud,
And at the sound it shrunk in haste away
And vanished from our sight.
HAMLET   'Tis very strange.
HORATIO
As I do live, my honored lord, 'tis true,
And we did think it writ down in our duty
To let you know of it.
HAMLET
Indeed, indeed, sirs, but this troubles me.
Hold you the watch to-night?
ALL   We do, my lord.
HAMLET Armed, say you?
ALL Armed, my lord.
HAMLET
From top to toe?
ALL   My lord, from head to foot.

---

204 *truncheon* military commander's baton   **216** *it* its

42

HAMLET
  Then saw you not his face?
HORATIO
  O, yes, my lord. He wore his beaver up.   230
HAMLET
  What, looked he frowningly?
HORATIO
  A countenance more in sorrow than in anger.
HAMLET Pale or red?
HORATIO
  Nay, very pale.
HAMLET   And fixed his eyes upon you?
HORATIO
  Most constantly.
HAMLET   I would I had been there.
HORATIO
  It would have much amazed you.
HAMLET
  Very like, very like. Stayed it long?
HORATIO
  While one with moderate haste might tell a hundred.   238
BOTH Longer, longer.
HORATIO
  Not when I saw't.
HAMLET   His beard was grizzled, no?   240
HORATIO
  It was as I have seen it in his life,
  A sable silvered.   242
HAMLET   I will watch to-night.
  Perchance 'twill walk again.
HORATIO   I warr'nt it will.
HAMLET
  If it assume my noble father's person,
  I'll speak to it though hell itself should gape

230 *beaver* visor or movable face-guard of the helmet   238 *tell* count   240
grizzled grey   242 *sable silvered* black mixed with white

And bid me hold my peace. I pray you all,
If you have hitherto concealed this sight,
248 Let it be tenable in your silence still,
And whatsomever else shall hap to-night,
Give it an understanding but no tongue.
I will requite your loves. So fare you well.
Upon the platform, 'twixt eleven and twelve
I'll visit you.

ALL   Our duty to your honor.

HAMLET
Your loves, as mine to you. Farewell.

                                   Exeunt [all but Hamlet].
My father's spirit – in arms ? All is not well.
256 I doubt some foul play. Would the night were come !
Till then sit still, my soul. Foul deeds will rise,
Though all the earth o'erwhelm them, to men's eyes.

                                              Exit.

                        *

I, iii   *Enter Laertes and Ophelia, his sister.*

LAERTES
My necessaries are embarked. Farewell.
And, sister, as the winds give benefit
3   And convoy is assistant, do not sleep,
But let me hear from you.

OPHELIA   Do you doubt that ?

LAERTES
For Hamlet, and the trifling of his favor,
Hold it a fashion and a toy in blood,
7   A violet in the youth of primy nature,
Forward, not permanent, sweet, not lasting,
9   The perfume and suppliance of a minute,
No more.

---

248 *tenable* held firmly   256 *doubt* suspect, fear
I, iii Elsinore Castle: the chambers of Polonius   3 *convoy* means of trans-
port   7 *primy* of the springtime   9 *perfume and suppliance* filling sweetness

OPHELIA No more but so?
LAERTES   Think it no more.
For nature crescent does not grow alone   11
In thews and bulk, but as this temple waxes   12
The inward service of the mind and soul
Grows wide withal. Perhaps he loves you now,
And now no soil nor cautel doth besmirch   15
The virtue of his will, but you must fear,   16
His greatness weighed, his will is not his own.   17
[For he himself is subject to his birth.]
He may not, as unvalued persons do,
Carve for himself, for on his choice depends
The safety and health of this whole state,
And therefore must his choice be circumscribed
Unto the voice and yielding of that body   23
Whereof he is the head. Then if he says he loves you,
It fits your wisdom so far to believe it
As he in his particular act and place
May give his saying deed, which is no further
Than the main voice of Denmark goes withal.
Then weigh what loss your honor may sustain
If with too credent ear you list his songs,   30
Or lose your heart, or your chaste treasure open
To his unmastered importunity.
Fear it, Ophelia, fear it, my dear sister,
And keep you in the rear of your affection,   34
Out of the shot and danger of desire.
The chariest maid is prodigal enough
If she unmask her beauty to the moon.
Virtue itself scapes not calumnious strokes.
The canker galls the infants of the spring   39
Too oft before their buttons be disclosed,   40
And in the morn and liquid dew of youth

11 *crescent* growing 12 *this temple* the body 15 *cautel* deceit 16 *will*
desire 17 *greatness weighed* high position considered 23 *yielding* assent
30 *credent* credulous 34 *affection* feelings, which rashly lead forward into
dangers 39 *canker* rose worm; *galls* injures 40 *buttons* buds

42   Contagious blastments are most imminent.
Be wary then ; best safety lies in fear.
Youth to itself rebels, though none else near.

OPHELIA

I shall the effect of this good lesson keep
As watchman to my heart, but, good my brother,
Do not as some ungracious pastors do,
Show me the steep and thorny way to heaven,
Whiles like a puffed and reckless libertine
Himself the primrose path of dalliance treads

51   And recks not his own rede.

       Enter Polonius.

LAERTES   O, fear me not.

I stay too long. But here my father comes.
A double blessing is a double grace ;
Occasion smiles upon a second leave.

POLONIUS

Yet here, Laertes ? Aboard, aboard, for shame !
The wind sits in the shoulder of your sail,
And you are stayed for. There – my blessing with thee,
And these few precepts in thy memory

59   Look thou character. Give thy thoughts no tongue,
60   Nor any unproportioned thought his act.
Be thou familiar, but by no means vulgar.
Those friends thou hast, and their adoption tried,
Grapple them unto thy soul with hoops of steel,
But do not dull thy palm with entertainment

65   Of each new-hatched, unfledged courage. Beware
Of entrance to a quarrel ; but being in,
Bear't that th' opposèd may beware of thee.
Give every man thine ear, but few thy voice ;

69   Take each man's censure, but reserve thy judgment.
Costly thy habit as thy purse can buy,
But not expressed in fancy ; rich, not gaudy,

---

42 *blastments* blights   51 *recks* regards; *rede* counsel   59 *character* inscribe
60 *unproportioned* unadjusted to what is right   65 *courage* man of spirit,
young blood   69 *censure* judgment

For the apparel oft proclaims the man,
And they in France of the best rank and station
Are of a most select and generous chief in that.   74
Neither a borrower nor a lender be,
For loan oft loses both itself and friend,
And borrowing dulleth edge of husbandry.   77
This above all, to thine own self be true,
And it must follow as the night the day
Thou canst not then be false to any man.
Farewell. My blessing season this in thee !   81

LAERTES
Most humbly do I take my leave, my lord.

POLONIUS
The time invites you. Go, your servants tend.   83

LAERTES
Farewell, Ophelia, and remember well
What I have said to you.

OPHELIA   'Tis in my memory locked,
And you yourself shall keep the key of it.

LAERTES Farewell.   *Exit Laertes.*

POLONIUS
What is't, Ophelia, he hath said to you ?

OPHELIA
So please you, something touching the Lord Hamlet.

POLONIUS
Marry, well bethought.   90
'Tis told me he hath very oft of late
Given private time to you, and you yourself
Have of your audience been most free and bounteous.
If it be so – as so 'tis put on me,
And that in way of caution – I must tell you
You do not understand yourself so clearly
As it behooves my daughter and your honor.
What is between you ? Give me up the truth.

74 *chief* eminence   77 *husbandry* thriftiness   81 *season* ripen and make
fruitful   83 *tend* wait   90 *Marry* by Mary

OPHELIA

99   He hath, my lord, of late made many tenders
      Of his affection to me.

POLONIUS

      Affection? Pooh! You speak like a green girl,
102   Unsifted in such perilous circumstance.
      Do you believe his tenders, as you call them?

OPHELIA

      I do not know, my lord, what I should think.

POLONIUS

      Marry, I will teach you. Think yourself a baby
106   That you have ta'en these tenders for true pay
      Which are not sterling. Tender yourself more dearly,
108   Or (not to crack the wind of the poor phrase,
      Running it thus) you'll tender me a fool.

OPHELIA

      My lord, he hath importuned me with love
      In honorable fashion.

POLONIUS

112   Ay, fashion you may call it. Go to, go to.

OPHELIA

      And hath given countenance to his speech, my lord,
      With almost all the holy vows of heaven.

POLONIUS

115   Ay, springes to catch woodcocks. I do know,
      When the blood burns, how prodigal the soul
      Lends the tongue vows. These blazes, daughter,
      Giving more light than heat, extinct in both

---

99 *tenders* offers   **102** *Unsifted* untested   **106–09** *tenders . . . Tender . . .
tender* offers . . . hold in regard . . . present (a word play going through three
meanings, the last use of the word yielding further complexity with its valid
implications that she will show herself to him as a fool, will show him to the
world as a fool, and may go so far as to present him with a baby, which would
be a fool because 'fool' was an Elizabethan term of endearment especially
applicable to an infant as a 'little innocent')   **108** *crack . . . of* make wheeze
like a horse driven too hard   **112** *Go to* go away, go on (expressing im-
patience)   **115** *springes* snares; *woodcocks* birds believed foolish

Even in their promise, as it is a-making,
You must not take for fire. From this time
Be something scanter of your maiden presence.
Set your entreatments at a higher rate   122
Than a command to parley. For Lord Hamlet,   123
Believe so much in him that he is young,
And with a larger tether may he walk
Than may be given you. In few, Ophelia,
Do not believe his vows, for they are brokers,   127
Not of that dye which their investments show,   128
But mere implorators of unholy suits,
Breathing like sanctified and pious bawds,
The better to beguile. This is for all :
I would not, in plain terms, from this time forth
Have you so slander any moment leisure   133
As to give words or talk with the Lord Hamlet.
Look to't, I charge you. Come your ways.

OPHELIA
I shall obey, my lord.   *Exeunt.*

*

Enter Hamlet, Horatio, and Marcellus.   I, iv

HAMLET
The air bites shrewdly ; it is very cold.   1

HORATIO
It is a nipping and an eager air.   2

HAMLET
What hour now ?

HORATIO   I think it lacks of twelve.

MARCELLUS No, it is struck.

HORATIO
Indeed ? I heard it not. It then draws near the season

---

122 *entreatments* military negotiations for surrender   123 *parley* confer with
a besieger   127 *brokers* middlemen, panders   128 *investments* clothes   133
slander use disgracefully ; *moment* momentary
I, iv The sentry-post   1 *shrewdly* wickedly   2 *eager* sharp

Wherein the spirit held his wont to walk.
A flourish of trumpets, and two pieces goes off.
What does this mean, my lord?

HAMLET

8   The king doth wake to-night and takes his rouse,
9   Keeps wassail, and the swaggering upspring reels,
10   And as he drains his draughts of Rhenish down
     The kettledrum and trumpet thus bray out
12   The triumph of his pledge.

HORATIO   Is it a custom?

HAMLET

Ay, marry, is't,
But to my mind, though I am native here
And to the manner born, it is a custom
16   More honored in the breach than the observance.
     This heavy-headed revel east and west
18   Makes us traduced and taxed of other nations.
19   They clepe us drunkards and with swinish phrase
20   Soil our addition, and indeed it takes
     From our achievements, though performed at height,
22   The pith and marrow of our attribute.
     So oft it chances in particular men
24   That (for some vicious mole of nature in them,
     As in their birth, wherein they are not guilty,
26   Since nature cannot choose his origin)
27   By the o'ergrowth of some complexion,
28   Oft breaking down the pales and forts of reason,
29   Or by some habit that too much o'erleavens
30   The form of plausive manners – that (these men

---

8 *rouse* carousal 9 *upspring* a German dance 10 *Rhenish* Rhine wine 12 *triumph* achievement, feat (in downing a cup of wine at one draught) 16 *More . . . observance* better broken than observed 18 *taxed of* censured by 19 *clepe* call 20 *addition* reputation, title added as a distinction 22 *attribute* reputation, what is attributed 24 *mole* blemish, flaw 26 *his* its 27 *complexion* part of the make-up, combination of humors 28 *pales* barriers, fences 29 *o'erleavens* works change throughout, as yeast ferments dough 30 *plausive* pleasing

Carrying, I say, the stamp of one defect,
Being nature's livery, or fortune's star)   32
Their virtues else, be they as pure as grace,
As infinite as man may undergo,
Shall in the general censure take corruption
From that particular fault. The dram of evil
Doth all the noble substance of a doubt,   37
To his own scandal.
          Enter Ghost.
HORATIO   Look, my lord, it comes.
HAMLET
Angels and ministers of grace defend us!
Be thou a spirit of health or goblin damned,   40
Bring with thee airs from heaven or blasts from hell,
Be thy intents wicked or charitable,
Thou com'st in such a questionable shape
That I will speak to thee. I'll call thee Hamlet,
King, father, royal Dane. O, answer me!
Let me not burst in ignorance, but tell
Why thy canonized bones, hearsèd in death,   47
Have burst their cerements, why the sepulchre   48
Wherein we saw thee quietly interred
Hath oped his ponderous and marble jaws
To cast thee up again. What may this mean
That thou, dead corse, again in complete steel,
Revisits thus the glimpses of the moon,
Making night hideous, and we fools of nature   54
So horridly to shake our disposition
With thoughts beyond the reaches of our souls?
Say, why is this? wherefore? what should we do?
          [Ghost] beckons.

32 *livery* characteristic equipment or provision; *star* make-up as formed by
stellar influence   37 *Doth . . . doubt* (see Appendix: Supplementary Notes)
40 *of health* sound, good; *goblin* fiend   47 *canonized* buried with the
established rites of the Church   48 *cerements* waxed grave-cloths   54 *fools
of nature* men made conscious of natural limitations by a supernatural
manifestation

HORATIO
It beckons you to go away with it,
As if it some impartment did desire
To you alone.

MARCELLUS   Look with what courteous action
It waves you to a more removèd ground.
But do not go with it.

HORATIO   No, by no means.

HAMLET
It will not speak. Then will I follow it.

HORATIO
Do not, my lord.

HAMLET   Why, what should be the fear?
I do not set my life at a pin's fee,
And for my soul, what can it do to that,
Being a thing immortal as itself?
It waves me forth again. I'll follow it.

HORATIO
What if it tempt you toward the flood, my lord,
Or to the dreadful summit of the cliff
71   That beetles o'er his base into the sea,
And there assume some other horrible form,
73   Which might deprive your sovereignty of reason
And draw you into madness? Think of it.
75   The very place puts toys of desperation,
Without more motive, into every brain
That looks so many fathoms to the sea
And hears it roar beneath.

HAMLET   It waves me still.
Go on. I'll follow thee.

MARCELLUS
You shall not go, my lord.

HAMLET   Hold off your hands.

HORATIO
Be ruled. You shall not go.

71 *beetles* juts out 73 *deprive* take away; *sovereignty of reason* state of being ruled by reason 75 *toys* fancies

HAMLET   My fate cries out
  And makes each petty artere in this body   82
  As hardy as the Nemean lion's nerve.   83
  Still am I called. Unhand me, gentlemen.
  By heaven, I'll make a ghost of him that lets me!   85
  I say, away! Go on. I'll follow thee.
                           Exit Ghost, and Hamlet.

HORATIO
  He waxes desperate with imagination.
MARCELLUS
  Let's follow. 'Tis not fit thus to obey him.
HORATIO
  Have after. To what issue will this come?
MARCELLUS
  Something is rotten in the state of Denmark.
HORATIO
  Heaven will direct it.
MARCELLUS   Nay, let's follow him.   *Exeunt.*

*

   Enter Ghost and Hamlet.   I, v
HAMLET
  Whither wilt thou lead me? Speak. I'll go no further.
GHOST
  Mark me.
HAMLET   I will.
GHOST   My hour is almost come,
  When I to sulph'rous and tormenting flames   3
  Must render up myself.
HAMLET   Alas, poor ghost!
GHOST
  Pity me not, but lend thy serious hearing

---

82 *artere* artery   83 *Nemean lion* a lion slain by Hercules in the performance
of one of his twelve labors; *nerve* sinew   85 *lets* hinders
I, v Another part of the fortifications   3 *flames* sufferings in purgatory (not
hell)

To what I shall unfold.

HAMLET   Speak. I am bound to hear.

GHOST
So art thou to revenge, when thou shalt hear.

HAMLET   What?

GHOST
I am thy father's spirit,
Doomed for a certain term to walk the night,
11   And for the day confined to fast in fires,
Till the foul crimes done in my days of nature
Are burnt and purged away. But that I am forbid
To tell the secrets of my prison house,
I could a tale unfold whose lightest word
Would harrow up thy soul, freeze thy young blood,
17   Make thy two eyes like stars start from their spheres,
Thy knotted and combinèd locks to part,
19   And each particular hair to stand an end
20   Like quills upon the fretful porpentine.
21   But this eternal blazon must not be
To ears of flesh and blood. List, list, O, list!
If thou didst ever thy dear father love –

HAMLET   O God!

GHOST
Revenge his foul and most unnatural murder.

HAMLET   Murder?

GHOST
Murder most foul, as in the best it is,
But this most foul, strange, and unnatural.

HAMLET
Haste me to know't, that I, with wings as swift
30   As meditation or the thoughts of love,
May sweep to my revenge.

GHOST   I find thee apt,

---

11 *fast* do penance   17 *spheres* transparent revolving shells in each of which,
according to the Ptolemaic astronomy, a planet or other heavenly body was
placed   19 *an* on   20 *porpentine* porcupine   21 *eternal blazon* revelation of
eternity   30 *meditation* thought

And duller shouldst thou be than the fat weed
That roots itself in ease on Lethe wharf,   33
Wouldst thou not stir in this. Now, Hamlet, hear.
'Tis given out that, sleeping in my orchard,
A serpent stung me. So the whole ear of Denmark
Is by a forgèd process of my death   37
Rankly abused. But know, thou noble youth,
The serpent that did sting thy father's life
Now wears his crown.

HAMLET   O my prophetic soul!
My uncle?

GHOST
Ay, that incestuous, that adulterate beast,   42
With witchcraft of his wit, with traitorous gifts –
O wicked wit and gifts, that have the power
So to seduce! – won to his shameful lust
The will of my most seeming-virtuous queen.
O Hamlet, what a falling-off was there,
From me, whose love was of that dignity
That it went hand in hand even with the vow
I made to her in marriage, and to decline
Upon a wretch whose natural gifts were poor
To those of mine!
But virtue, as it never will be moved,
Though lewdness court it in a shape of heaven,   54
So lust, though to a radiant angel linked,
Will sate itself in a celestial bed
And prey on garbage.
But soft, methinks I scent the morning air.
Brief let me be. Sleeping within my orchard,
My custom always of the afternoon,
Upon my secure hour thy uncle stole   61
With juice of cursed hebona in a vial,   62

---

33 *Lethe* the river in Hades which brings forgetfulness of past life to a spirit
who drinks of it   37 *forgèd process* falsified official report   42 *adulterate*
adulterous   54 *shape of heaven* angelic disguise   61 *secure* carefree, un-
suspecting   62 *hebona* some poisonous plant

And in the porches of my ears did pour
The leperous distilment, whose effect
Holds such an enmity with blood of man
That swift as quicksilver it courses through
The natural gates and alleys of the body,
68 And with a sudden vigor it doth posset
69 And curd, like eager droppings into milk,
The thin and wholesome blood. So did it mine,
71 And a most instant tetter barked about
72 Most lazar-like with vile and loathsome crust
All my smooth body.
Thus was I sleeping by a brother's hand
Of life, of crown, of queen at once dispatched,
Cut off even in the blossoms of my sin,
77 Unhouseled, disappointed, unaneled,
No reck'ning made, but sent to my account
With all my imperfections on my head.
O, horrible! O, horrible! most horrible!
If thou hast nature in thee, bear it not.
Let not the royal bed of Denmark be
83 A couch for luxury and damnèd incest.
But howsomever thou pursues this act,
Taint not thy mind, nor let thy soul contrive
Against thy mother aught. Leave her to heaven
And to those thorns that in her bosom lodge
To prick and sting her. Fare thee well at once.
89 The glowworm shows the matin to be near
And gins to pale his uneffectual fire.
Adieu, adieu, adieu. Remember me.   *[Exit.]*
HAMLET
O all you host of heaven! O earth! What else?
And shall I couple hell? O fie! Hold, hold, my heart,

68 *posset* curdle   69 *eager* sour   71 *tetter* eruption; *barked* covered as with a bark   72 *lazar-like* leper-like   77 *Unhouseled* without the Sacrament; *disappointed* unprepared spiritually; *unaneled* without extreme unction   83 *luxury* lust   89 *matin* morning

And you, my sinews, grow not instant old,
But bear me stiffly up. Remember thee?
Ay, thou poor ghost, while memory holds a seat
In this distracted globe. Remember thee?   97
Yea, from the table of my memory   98
I'll wipe away all trivial fond records,
All saws of books, all forms, all pressures past   100
That youth and observation copied there,
And thy commandment all alone shall live
Within the book and volume of my brain,
Unmixed with baser matter. Yes, by heaven!
O most pernicious woman!
O villain, villain, smiling, damnèd villain!
My tables – meet it is I set it down
That one may smile, and smile, and be a villain.
At least I am sure it may be so in Denmark.
    [Writes.]
So, uncle, there you are. Now to my word:
It is 'Adieu, adieu, remember me.'
I have sworn't.
    Enter Horatio and Marcellus.

HORATIO
My lord, my lord!
MARCELLUS   Lord Hamlet!
HORATIO   Heavens secure him!
HAMLET So be it!
MARCELLUS
Illo, ho, ho, my lord!
HAMLET   115
Hillo, ho, ho, boy! Come, bird, come.
MARCELLUS
How is't, my noble lord?
HORATIO   What news, my lord?

97 *globe* head   **98** *table* writing tablet, record book   **100** *saws* wise sayings;
forms mental images, concepts; *pressures* impressions   **115** *Illo, ho, ho* cry of
the falconer to summon his hawk

HAMLET O, wonderful!

HORATIO
Good my lord, tell it.

HAMLET   No, you will reveal it.

HORATIO
Not I, my lord, by heaven.

MARCELLUS   Nor I, my lord.

HAMLET
How say you then? Would heart of man once think it?
But you'll be secret?

BOTH   Ay, by heaven, my lord.

HAMLET
There's never a villain dwelling in all Denmark
But he's an arrant knave.

HORATIO
There needs no ghost, my lord, come from the grave
To tell us this.

HAMLET   Why, right, you are in the right,
127   And so, without more circumstance at all,
I hold it fit that we shake hands and part:
You, as your business and desires shall point you,
For every man hath business and desire
Such as it is, and for my own poor part,
Look you, I'll go pray.

HORATIO
These are but wild and whirling words, my lord.

HAMLET
I am sorry they offend you, heartily;
Yes, faith, heartily.

HORATIO   There's no offense, my lord.

HAMLET
Yes, by Saint Patrick, but there is, Horatio,
And much offense too. Touching this vision here,
138   It is an honest ghost, that let me tell you.
For your desire to know what is between us,

127 *circumstance* ceremony   138 *honest* genuine (not a disguised demon)

O'ermaster't as you may. And now, good friends,
As you are friends, scholars, and soldiers,
Give me one poor request.

HORATIO
What is't, my lord? We will.

HAMLET
Never make known what you have seen to-night.

BOTH
My lord, we will not.

HAMLET   Nay, but swear't.

HORATIO   In faith,
My lord, not I.

MARCELLUS   Nor I, my lord – in faith.

HAMLET
Upon my sword.   147

MARCELLUS   We have sworn, my lord, already.

HAMLET
Indeed, upon my sword, indeed.
          Ghost cries under the stage.

GHOST Swear.

HAMLET
Ha, ha, boy, say'st thou so? Art thou there, truepenny? 150
Come on. You hear this fellow in the cellarage.
Consent to swear.

HORATIO   Propose the oath, my lord.

HAMLET
Never to speak of this that you have seen,
Swear by my sword.

GHOST *[beneath]* Swear.

HAMLET
Hic et ubique? Then we'll shift our ground.   156
Come hither, gentlemen,
And lay your hands again upon my sword.
Swear by my sword

---

147 *sword* i.e. upon the cross formed by the sword hilt   **150** *truepenny* honest
old fellow   **156** *Hic et ubique* here and everywhere

Never to speak of this that you have heard.
GHOST [beneath] Swear by his sword.
HAMLET
   Well said, old mole ! Canst work i' th' earth so fast ?
163 A worthy pioner ! Once more remove, good friends.
HORATIO
   O day and night, but this is wondrous strange !
HAMLET
   And therefore as a stranger give it welcome.
   There are more things in heaven and earth, Horatio,
167 Than are dreamt of in your philosophy.
   But come :
   Here as before, never, so help you mercy,
   How strange or odd some'er I bear myself
   (As I perchance hereafter shall think meet
172 To put an antic disposition on),
   That you, at such times seeing me, never shall,
174 With arms encumb'red thus, or this head-shake,
   Or by pronouncing of some doubtful phrase,
176 As 'Well, well, we know,' or 'We could, an if we would,'
   Or 'If we list to speak,' or 'There be, an if they might,'
   Or such ambiguous giving out, to note
   That you know aught of me – this do swear,
   So grace and mercy at your most need help you.
GHOST [beneath] Swear.
     [They swear.]
HAMLET
   Rest, rest, perturbèd spirit ! So, gentlemen,
183 With all my love I do commend me to you,
   And what so poor a man as Hamlet is
   May do t' express his love and friending to you,
   God willing, shall not lack. Let us go in together,
187 And still your fingers on your lips, I pray.

163 *pioner* pioneer, miner   167 *your philosophy* this philosophy one hears
about   172 *antic* grotesque, mad   174 *encumb'red* folded   176 *an if* if   183
commend entrust   187 *still* always

The time is out of joint. O cursèd spite
That ever I was born to set it right!
Nay, come, let's go together.   *Exeunt.*

*

Enter old Polonius, with his man [Reynaldo].   II, i

POLONIUS
  Give him this money and these notes, Reynaldo.
REYNALDO
  I will, my lord.
POLONIUS
  You shall do marvellous wisely, good Reynaldo,
  Before you visit him, to make inquire
  Of his behavior.
REYNALDO   My lord, I did intend it.
POLONIUS
  Marry, well said, very well said. Look you, sir,
  Enquire me first what Danskers are in Paris,   7
  And how, and who, what means, and where they keep,   8
  What company, at what expense; and finding
  By this encompassment and drift of question   10
  That they do know my son, come you more nearer
  Than your particular demands will touch it.   12
  Take you as 'twere some distant knowledge of him,
  As thus, 'I know his father and his friends,
  And in part him' – do you mark this, Reynaldo?
REYNALDO
  Ay, very well, my lord.
POLONIUS
  'And in part him, but,' you may say, 'not well,
  But if't be he I mean, he's very wild
  Addicted so and so.' And there put on him

II, i *The chambers of Polonius*   7 *Danskers* Danes   8 *what means* what their
wealth; *keep* dwell   10 *encompassment* circling about   12 *particular demands* definite questions

61

20   What forgeries you please ; marry, none so rank
        As may dishonor him – take heed of that –
        But, sir, such wanton, wild, and usual slips
        As are companions noted and most known
        To youth and liberty.

REYNALDO   As gaming, my lord.

POLONIUS
        Ay, or drinking, fencing, swearing, quarrelling,
26   Drabbing. You may go so far.

REYNALDO
        My lord, that would dishonor him.

POLONIUS
28   Faith, no, as you may season it in the charge.
        You must not put another scandal on him,
30   That he is open to incontinency.
31   That's not my meaning. But breathe his faults so quaintly
        That they may seem the taints of liberty,
        The flash and outbreak of a fiery mind,
34   A savageness in unreclaimèd blood,
35   Of general assault.

REYNALDO   But, my good lord –

POLONIUS
        Wherefore should you do this ?

REYNALDO   Ay, my lord,
        I would know that.

POLONIUS   Marry, sir, here's my drift,
38   And I believe it is a fetch of warrant.
        You laying these slight sullies on my son
        As 'twere a thing a little soiled i' th' working,
        Mark you,
        Your party in converse, him you would sound,

---

20 *forgeries* invented wrongdoings   26 *Drabbing* whoring   28 *season* soften
30 *incontinency* extreme sensuality   31 *quaintly* expertly, gracefully   34
unreclaimèd untamed   35 *Of general assault* assailing all young men   38
fetch of warrant allowable trick

Having ever seen in the prenominate crimes 43
The youth you breathe of guilty, be assured
He closes with you in this consequence: 45
'Good sir,' or so, or 'friend,' or 'gentleman' –
According to the phrase or the addition 47
Of man and country –

REYNALDO   Very good, my lord.

POLONIUS
And then, sir, does 'a this – 'a does –
What was I about to say? By the mass, I was about to
say something! Where did I leave?

REYNALDO At 'closes in the consequence,' at 'friend or
so,' and 'gentleman.'

POLONIUS
At 'closes in the consequence' – Ay, marry!
He closes thus: 'I know the gentleman;
I saw him yesterday, or t' other day,
Or then, or then, with such or such, and, as you say,
There was 'a gaming, there o'ertook in's rouse, 58
There falling out at tennis'; or perchance, 59
'I saw him enter such a house of sale,'
Videlicet, a brothel, or so forth. 61
See you now –
Your bait of falsehood takes this carp of truth,
And thus do we of wisdom and of reach, 64
With windlasses and with assays of bias, 65
By indirections find directions out. 66
So, by my former lecture and advice,
Shall you my son. You have me, have you not?

---

43 *Having ever* if he has ever; *prenominate* aforementioned 45 *closes with you* follows your lead to a conclusion; *consequence* following way 47 *addition* title 58 *o'ertook* overcome with drunkenness; *rouse* carousal 59 *falling out* quarrelling 61 *Videlicet* namely 64 *reach* far-reaching comprehension 65 *windlasses* roundabout courses; *assays of bias* devious attacks 66 *directions* ways of procedure

REYNALDO
My lord, I have.

69 POLONIUS   God bye ye, fare ye well.

REYNALDO Good my lord.

POLONIUS
Observe his inclination in yourself.

REYNALDO I shall, my lord.

POLONIUS
And let him ply his music.

REYNALDO   Well, my lord.

POLONIUS
Farewell.   *Exit Reynaldo.*
          Enter Ophelia.
               How now, Ophelia, what's the matter?

OPHELIA
O my lord, my lord, I have been so affrighted!

POLONIUS
With what, i' th' name of God?

OPHELIA
77 My lord, as I was sewing in my closet,
78 Lord Hamlet, with his doublet all unbraced,
    No hat upon his head, his stockings fouled,
80 Ungartered, and down-gyvèd to his ankle,
    Pale as his shirt, his knees knocking each other,
    And with a look so piteous in purport
    As if he had been loosèd out of hell
    To speak of horrors – he comes before me.

POLONIUS
Mad for thy love?

OPHELIA   My lord, I do not know,
But truly I do fear it.

POLONIUS   What said he?

OPHELIA
He took me by the wrist and held me hard.

69 *God bye ye* God be with you, good-bye   77 *closet* private living-room
78 *doublet* jacket; *unbraced* unlaced   80 *down-gyvèd* fallen down like gyves
or fetters on a prisoner's legs

Then goes he to the length of all his arm,
And with his other hand thus o'er his brow
He falls to such perusal of my face   90
As 'a would draw it. Long stayed he so.
At last, a little shaking of mine arm
And thrice his head thus waving up and down,
He raised a sigh so piteous and profound
As it did seem to shatter all his bulk
And end his being. That done, he lets me go,
And with his head over his shoulder turned
He seemed to find his way without his eyes,
For out o' doors he went without their helps
And to the last bended their light on me.

POLONIUS
Come, go with me. I will go seek the king.
This is the very ecstasy of love,   102
Whose violent property fordoes itself   103
And leads the will to desperate undertakings
As oft as any passion under heaven
That does afflict our natures. I am sorry.
What, have you given him any hard words of late?

OPHELIA
No, my good lord; but as you did command
I did repel his letters and denied
His access to me.

POLONIUS   That hath made him mad.
I am sorry that with better heed and judgment
I had not quoted him. I feared he did but trifle   112
And meant to wrack thee; but beshrew my jealousy.   113
By heaven, it is as proper to our age
To cast beyond ourselves in our opinions   115
As it is common for the younger sort
To lack discretion. Come, go we to the king.

---

102 *ecstasy* madness   103 *property* quality; *fordoes* destroys   112 *quoted*
observed   113 *beshrew* curse   115 *cast beyond ourselves* find by calculation
more significance in something than we ought to

118   This must be known, which, being kept close, might
          move
119   More grief to hide than hate to utter love.
          Come.   *Exeunt.*

                                              *

II, ii   *Flourish. Enter King and Queen, Rosencrantz, and*
                Guildenstern [with others].

    KING
          Welcome, dear Rosencrantz and Guildenstern.
2   Moreover that we much did long to see you,
          The need we have to use you did provoke
          Our hasty sending. Something have you heard
          Of Hamlet's transformation – so call it,
6   Sith nor th' exterior nor the inward man
          Resembles that it was. What it should be,
          More than his father's death, that thus hath put him
          So much from th' understanding of himself,
          I cannot dream of. I entreat you both
          That, being of so young days brought up with him,
12   And sith so neighbored to his youth and havior,
          That you vouchsafe your rest here in our court
          Some little time, so by your companies
          To draw him on to pleasures, and to gather
          So much as from occasion you may glean,
          Whether aught to us unknown afflicts him thus,
18   That opened lies within our remedy.
    QUEEN
          Good gentlemen, he hath much talked of you,
          And sure I am two men there are not living
21   To whom he more adheres. If it will please you

---

118 *close* secret; *move* cause   119 *to hide . . . love* by such hiding of love than
there would be hate moved by a revelation of it (a violently condensed put-
ting of the case which is a triumph of special statement for Polonius)
II, ii A chamber in the Castle   2 *Moreover that* besides the fact that   6
Sith since   12 *youth and havior* youthful ways of life   18 *opened* revealed
21 *more adheres* is more attached

To show us so much gentry and good will 22
As to expend your time with us awhile
For the supply and profit of our hope,
Your visitation shall receive such thanks
As fits a king's remembrance.

ROSENCRANTZ   Both your majesties
Might, by the sovereign power you have of us,
Put your dread pleasures more into command
Than to entreaty.

GUILDENSTERN   But we both obey,
And here give up ourselves in the full bent 30
To lay our service freely at your feet,
To be commanded.

KING
Thanks, Rosencrantz and gentle Guildenstern.

QUEEN
Thanks, Guildenstern and gentle Rosencrantz.
And I beseech you instantly to visit
My too much changèd son. – Go, some of you,
And bring these gentlemen where Hamlet is.

GUILDENSTERN
Heavens make our presence and our practices
Pleasant and helpful to him!

QUEEN   Ay, amen!
        Exeunt Rosencrantz and Guildenstern
            [with some Attendants].

     Enter Polonius.

POLONIUS
Th' ambassadors from Norway, my good lord,
Are joyfully returned.

KING
Thou still hast been the father of good news. 42

POLONIUS
Have I, my lord? Assure you, my good liege,

---

22 *gentry* courtesy   30 *in the full bent* at the limit of bending (of a bow), to
full capacity   42 *still* always

I hold my duty as I hold my soul,
Both to my God and to my gracious king,
And I do think – or else this brain of mine
Hunts not the trail of policy so sure
As it hath used to do – that I have found
The very cause of Hamlet's lunacy.

KING

O, speak of that! That do I long to hear.

POLONIUS

Give first admittance to th' ambassadors.

52 My news shall be the fruit to that great feast.

KING

53 Thyself do grace to them and bring them in.

[Exit Polonius.]

He tells me, my dear Gertrude, he hath found
The head and source of all your son's distemper.

QUEEN

56 I doubt it is no other but the main,
His father's death and our o'erhasty marriage.

KING

Well, we shall sift him.

Enter Ambassadors [Voltemand and Cornelius,
with Polonius].   Welcome, my good friends.
Say, Voltemand, what from our brother Norway?

VOLTEMAND

Most fair return of greetings and desires.

61 Upon our first, he sent out to suppress
His nephew's levies, which to him appeared
To be a preparation 'gainst the Polack,
But better looked into, he truly found
It was against your highness, whereat grieved,
That so his sickness, age, and impotence

67 Was falsely borne in hand, sends out arrests
On Fortinbras; which he in brief obeys,

---

52 *fruit* dessert   **53** *grace* honor   **56** *doubt* suspect   **61** *our first* our first
words about the matter   **67** *borne in hand* deceived

Receives rebuke from Norway, and in fine   69
Makes vow before his uncle never more
To give th' assay of arms against your majesty.   71
Whereon old Norway, overcome with joy,
Gives him threescore thousand crowns in annual fee
And his commission to employ those soldiers,
So levied as before, against the Polack,
With an entreaty, herein further shown,
    [Gives a paper.]
That it might please you to give quiet pass
Through your dominions for this enterprise,
On such regards of safety and allowance   79
As therein are set down.

KING   It likes us well ;
And at our more considered time we'll read,   81
Answer, and think upon this business.
Meantime we thank you for your well-took labor.
Go to your rest ; at night we'll feast together.
Most welcome home !   *Exeunt Ambassadors.*

POLONIUS   This business is well ended.
My liege and madam, to expostulate   86
What majesty should be, what duty is,
Why day is day, night night, and time is time,
Were nothing but to waste night, day, and time.
Therefore, since brevity is the soul of wit,   90
And tediousness the limbs and outward flourishes,
I will be brief. Your noble son is mad.
Mad call I it, for, to define true madness,
What is't but to be nothing else but mad ?
But let that go.

QUEEN   More matter, with less art.
POLONIUS
Madam, I swear I use no art at all.
That he is mad, 'tis true : 'tis true 'tis pity,

---

69 *in fine* in the end   71 *assay* trial   79 *regards* terms   81 *considered time*
convenient time for consideration   86 *expostulate* discuss   90 *wit* understanding

98   And pity 'tis 'tis true – a foolish figure.
     But farewell it, for I will use no art.
     Mad let us grant him then, and now remains
     That we find out the cause of this effect –
     Or rather say, the cause of this defect,
     For this effect defective comes by cause.
     Thus it remains, and the remainder thus.

105   Perpend.
     I have a daughter (have while she is mine),
     Who in her duty and obedience, mark,
     Hath given me this. Now gather, and surmise.
        [Reads the] letter.
     'To the celestial, and my soul's idol, the most beautified
     Ophelia,' –
     That's an ill phrase, a vile phrase; 'beautified' is a vile
     phrase. But you shall hear. Thus:
        [Reads.]
     'In her excellent white bosom, these, &c.'

QUEEN
     Came this from Hamlet to her?

POLONIUS
     Good madam, stay awhile. I will be faithful.
        [Reads.]
        'Doubt thou the stars are fire;
         Doubt that the sun doth move;
118   Doubt truth to be a liar;
         But never doubt I love.
120   'O dear Ophelia, I am ill at these numbers. I have not
     art to reckon my groans, but that I love thee best, O
     most best, believe it. Adieu.
        'Thine evermore, most dear lady,
124   whilst this machine is to him, Hamlet.'

     This in obedience hath my daughter shown me,

---

98 *figure* figure in rhetoric   105 *Perpend* ponder   118 *Doubt* suspect   120 *numbers* verses   124 *machine* body; *to* attached to

And more above hath his solicitings,   126
As they fell out by time, by means, and place,
All given to mine ear.

KING   But how hath she
Received his love?

POLONIUS   What do you think of me?

KING
As of a man faithful and honorable.

POLONIUS
I would fain prove so. But what might you think,
When I had seen this hot love on the wing
(As I perceived it, I must tell you that,
Before my daughter told me), what might you,
Or my dear majesty your queen here, think,
If I had played the desk or table book,   136
Or given my heart a winking, mute and dumb,   137
Or looked upon this love with idle sight?
What might you think? No, I went round to work   139
And my young mistress thus I did bespeak:
'Lord Hamlet is a prince, out of thy star.   141
This must not be.' And then I prescripts gave her,   142
That she should lock herself from his resort,
Admit no messengers, receive no tokens.
Which done, she took the fruits of my advice,
And he, repellèd, a short tale to make,
Fell into a sadness, then into a fast,
Thence to a watch, thence into a weakness,   148
Thence to a lightness, and, by this declension,   149
Into the madness wherein now he raves,
And all we mourn for.

KING   Do you think 'tis this?

QUEEN
It may be, very like.

---

126 *above* besides   136 *desk or table book* i.e. silent receiver   137 *winking*
closing of the eyes   139 *round* roundly, plainly   141 *star* condition
determined by stellar influence   142 *prescripts* instructions   148 *watch*
sleepless state   149 *lightness* lightheadedness

POLONIUS
Hath there been such a time – I would fain know that –
That I have positively said ''Tis so,'
When it proved otherwise?

KING   Not that I know.

POLONIUS [pointing to his head and shoulder]
Take this from this, if this be otherwise.
If circumstances lead me, I will find
Where truth is hid, though it were hid indeed
159   Within the center.

KING   How may we try it further?

POLONIUS
You know sometimes he walks four hours together
Here in the lobby.

QUEEN   So he does indeed.

POLONIUS
At such a time I'll loose my daughter to him.
163   Be you and I behind an arras then.
Mark the encounter. If he love her not,
165   And be not from his reason fallen thereon,
Let me be no assistant for a state
But keep a farm and carters.

KING   We will try it.

Enter Hamlet [reading on a book].

QUEEN
But look where sadly the poor wretch comes reading.

POLONIUS
Away, I do beseech you both, away.
                        Exit King and Queen [with Attendants].
170   I'll board him presently. O, give me leave.
How does my good Lord Hamlet?

172 HAMLET Well, God-a-mercy.

POLONIUS Do you know me, my lord?

---

159 *center* center of the earth and also of the Ptolemaic universe   163 *arras*
hanging tapestry   165 *thereon* on that account   170 *board* accost; *presently*
at once   172 *God-a-mercy* thank you (literally, 'God have mercy!')

HAMLET Excellent well. You are a fishmonger.   174

POLONIUS Not I, my lord.

HAMLET Then I would you were so honest a man.

POLONIUS Honest, my lord?

HAMLET Ay, sir. To be honest, as this world goes, is to be one man picked out of ten thousand.

POLONIUS That's very true, my lord.

HAMLET For if the sun breed maggots in a dead dog, being a good kissing carrion – Have you a daughter?   182

POLONIUS I have, my lord.

HAMLET Let her not walk i' th' sun. Conception is a blessing, but as your daughter may conceive, friend, look to't.

POLONIUS *[aside]* How say you by that? Still harping on my daughter. Yet he knew me not at first. 'A said I was a fishmonger. 'A is far gone, far gone. And truly in my youth I suffered much extremity for love, very near this. I'll speak to him again. – What do you read, my lord?

HAMLET Words, words, words.

POLONIUS What is the matter, my lord?

HAMLET Between who?   193

POLONIUS I mean the matter that you read, my lord.

HAMLET Slanders, sir, for the satirical rogue says here that old men have grey beards, that their faces are wrinkled, their eyes purging thick amber and plum-tree gum, and that they have a plentiful lack of wit, together with most weak hams. All which, sir, though I most powerfully and potently believe, yet I hold it not honesty to have it thus set down, for you yourself, sir, should be old as I am if, like a crab, you could go backward.

POLONIUS *[aside]* Though this be madness, yet there is method in't. – Will you walk out of the air, my lord?

174 *fishmonger* seller of harlots, procurer (a cant term used here with a glance at the fishing Polonius is doing when he offers Ophelia as bait)   182 *good kissing carrion* good bit of flesh for kissing   193 *Between who* matter for a quarrel between what persons (Hamlet's willful misunderstanding)

HAMLET Into my grave?

206 POLONIUS Indeed, that's out of the air. *[aside]* How preg-
207 nant sometimes his replies are! a happiness that often
madness hits on, which reason and sanity could not so
prosperously be delivered of. I will leave him and suddenly contrive the means of meeting between him and
my daughter. – My honorable lord, I will most humbly
take my leave of you.

HAMLET You cannot, sir, take from me anything that I
214 will more willingly part withal – except my life, except
my life, except my life.
     Enter Guildenstern and Rosencrantz.

POLONIUS Fare you well, my lord.

HAMLET These tedious old fools!

POLONIUS You go to seek the Lord Hamlet. There he is.

ROSENCRANTZ *[to Polonius]* God save you, sir!
                         [Exit Polonius.]

GUILDENSTERN My honored lord!

ROSENCRANTZ My most dear lord!

HAMLET My excellent good friends! How dost thou,
Guildenstern? Ah, Rosencrantz! Good lads, how do ye
both?

ROSENCRANTZ
224 As the indifferent children of the earth.

GUILDENSTERN
Happy in that we are not over-happy.
On Fortune's cap we are not the very button.

HAMLET Nor the soles of her shoe?

ROSENCRANTZ Neither, my lord.

HAMLET Then you live about her waist, or in the middle
of her favors?

231 GUILDENSTERN Faith, her privates we.

HAMLET In the secret parts of Fortune? O, most true!
she is a strumpet. What news?

---

206 *pregnant* full of meaning   **207** *happiness* aptness of expression   **214**
withal with   **224** *indifferent* average   **231** *privates* ordinary men in private,
not public, life (with obvious play upon the sexual term 'private parts')

ROSENCRANTZ None, my lord, but that the world 's
    grown honest.

HAMLET Then is doomsday near. But your news is not
    true. [Let me question more in particular. What have
    you, my good friends, deserved at the hands of Fortune
    that she sends you to prison hither?

GUILDENSTERN Prison, my lord?

HAMLET Denmark 's a prison.

ROSENCRANTZ Then is the world one.

HAMLET A goodly one; in which there are many con-   243
    fines, wards, and dungeons, Denmark being one o' th'   244
    worst.

ROSENCRANTZ We think not so, my lord.

HAMLET Why, then 'tis none to you, for there is nothing
    either good or bad but thinking makes it so. To me it is a
    prison.

ROSENCRANTZ Why, then your ambition makes it one.
    'Tis too narrow for your mind.

HAMLET O God, I could be bounded in a nutshell and
    count myself a king of infinite space, were it not that I
    have bad dreams.

GUILDENSTERN Which dreams indeed are ambition, for
    the very substance of the ambitious is merely the
    shadow of a dream.

HAMLET A dream itself is but a shadow.

ROSENCRANTZ Truly, and I hold ambition of so airy and
    light a quality that it is but a shadow's shadow.

HAMLET Then are our beggars bodies, and our monarchs   260
    and outstretched heroes the beggars' shadows. Shall we   261
    to th' court? for, by my fay, I cannot reason.   262

BOTH We'll wait upon you.   263

HAMLET No such matter. I will not sort you with the rest

---

243 *confines* places of imprisonment   244 *wards* cells   260 *bodies* solid
substances, not shadows (because beggars lack ambition)   261 *outstretched*
elongated as shadows (with a corollary implication of far-reaching with
respect to the ambitions that make both heroes and monarchs into shadows)
262 *fay* faith   263 *wait upon* attend

of my servants, for, to speak to you like an honest man, I
am most dreadfully attended.] But in the beaten way of
267   friendship, what make you at Elsinore?

ROSENCRANTZ To visit you, my lord; no other occasion.

HAMLET Beggar that I am, I am even poor in thanks, but
I thank you; and sure, dear friends, my thanks are too
271   dear a halfpenny. Were you not sent for? Is it your own
inclining? Is it a free visitation? Come, come, deal
justly with me. Come, come. Nay, speak.

GUILDENSTERN What should we say, my lord?

HAMLET Why, anything – but to th' purpose. You were
sent for, and there is a kind of confession in your looks,
which your modesties have not craft enough to color.
I know the good king and queen have sent for you.

ROSENCRANTZ To what end, my lord?

HAMLET That you must teach me. But let me conjure you
281   by the rights of our fellowship, by the consonancy of our
youth, by the obligation of our ever-preserved love, and
283   by what more dear a better proposer can charge you
284   withal, be even and direct with me whether you were
sent for or no.

ROSENCRANTZ [aside to Guildenstern] What say you?

HAMLET [aside] Nay then, I have an eye of you. – If you
love me, hold not off.

GUILDENSTERN My lord, we were sent for.

290 HAMLET I will tell you why. So shall my anticipation pre-
291   vent your discovery, and your secrecy to the king and
292   queen moult no feather. I have of late – but wherefore I
know not – lost all my mirth, forgone all custom of ex-
ercises; and indeed, it goes so heavily with my disposition that this goodly frame the earth seems to me a sterile
promontory; this most excellent canopy, the air, look
297   you, this brave o'erhanging firmament, this majestical

267 *make* do   271 *a halfpenny* at a halfpenny   281 *consonancy* accord (in
sameness of age)   283 *proposer* propounder   284 *withal* with; *even* straight
290 *prevent* forestall   291 *discovery* disclosure   292 *moult no feather* be left
whole   297 *firmament* sky

roof fretted with golden fire – why, it appeareth nothing 298
to me but a foul and pestilent congregation of vapors.
What a piece of work is a man, how noble in reason,
how infinite in faculties; in form and moving how ex- 301
press and admirable, in action how like an angel, in apprehension how like a god: the beauty of the world, the
paragon of animals! And yet to me what is this quint- 304
essence of dust? Man delights not me – nor woman
neither, though by your smiling you seem to say so.

ROSENCRANTZ My lord, there was no such stuff in my
thoughts.

HAMLET Why did ye laugh then, when I said 'Man delights not me'?

ROSENCRANTZ To think, my lord, if you delight not in
man, what lenten entertainment the players shall re- 311
ceive from you. We coted them on the way, and hither 312
are they coming to offer you service.

HAMLET He that plays the king shall be welcome – his
majesty shall have tribute of me – , the adventurous
knight shall use his foil and target, the lover shall not 316
sigh gratis, the humorous man shall end his part in 317
peace, the clown shall make those laugh whose lungs are
tickle o' th' sere, and the lady shall say her mind freely, 319
or the blank verse shall halt for't. What players are 320
they?

ROSENCRANTZ Even those you were wont to take such
delight in, the tragedians of the city.

HAMLET How chances it they travel? Their residence, 323
both in reputation and profit, was better both ways.

ROSENCRANTZ I think their inhibition comes by the 325

298 *fretted* decorated with fretwork   301 *express* well framed   304 *quintessence* fifth or last and finest essence (an alchemical term)   311 *lenten* scanty
312 *coted* overtook   316 *foil and target* sword and shield   317 *humorous man*
eccentric character dominated by one of the humours   319 *tickle o' th' sere*
hair-triggered for the discharge of laughter ('sere': part of a gunlock)   320
halt go lame   323 *residence* residing at the capital   325 *inhibition* impedi-
ment to acting in residence (formal prohibition?)

326   means of the late innovation.

HAMLET Do they hold the same estimation they did when
I was in the city? Are they so followed?

ROSENCRANTZ No indeed, are they not.

[**HAMLET** How comes it? Do they grow rusty?

ROSENCRANTZ Nay, their endeavor keeps in the wonted
332   pace, but there is, sir, an eyrie of children, little eyases,
333   that cry out on the top of question and are most tyran-
nically clapped for't. These are now the fashion, and so
335   berattle the common stages (so they call them) that
336   many wearing rapiers are afraid of goosequills and dare
scarce come thither.

HAMLET What, are they children? Who maintains 'em?
339   How are they escoted? Will they pursue the quality no
340   longer than they can sing? Will they not say afterwards,
if they should grow themselves to common players (as it
is most like, if their means are no better), their writers
do them wrong to make them exclaim against their own
succession?

ROSENCRANTZ Faith, there has been much to do on both
346   sides, and the nation holds it no sin to tarre them to con-
347   troversy. There was, for a while, no money bid for argument unless the poet and the player went to cuffs in the
question.

HAMLET Is't possible?

GUILDENSTERN O, there has been much throwing about
of brains.

HAMLET Do the boys carry it away?

---

326 *innovation* new fashion of having companies of boy actors play on the
'private' stage (?), political upheaval (?)   332 *eyrie* nest; *eyases* nestling
hawks   333 *on the top of question* above others on matter of dispute   335 *berattle* berate; *common stages* 'public' theatres of the 'common' players, who
were organized in companies mainly composed of adult actors (allusion
being made to the 'War of the Theatres' in Shakespeare's London)   336
goosequills pens (of satirists who made out that the London public stage
showed low taste)   339 *escoted* supported; *quality* profession of acting   340
sing i.e. with unchanged voices   346 *tarre* incite   347 *argument* matter of a
play

ROSENCRANTZ Ay, that they do, my lord – Hercules and
 his load too.]   354

HAMLET It is not very strange, for my uncle is King of
 Denmark, and those that would make mows at him   356
 while my father lived give twenty, forty, fifty, a hundred
 ducats apiece for his picture in little. 'Sblood, there is   358
 something in this more than natural, if philosophy
 could find it out.

 A flourish.

GUILDENSTERN There are the players.

HAMLET Gentlemen, you are welcome to Elsinore. Your
 hands, come then. Th' appurtenance of welcome is
 fashion and ceremony. Let me comply with you in this
 garb, lest my extent to the players (which I tell you must 364
 show fairly outwards) should more appear like entertainment than yours. You are welcome. But my uncle-
 father and aunt-mother are deceived.

GUILDENSTERN In what, my dear lord?

HAMLET I am but mad north-north-west. When the
 wind is southerly I know a hawk from a handsaw.   370

 Enter Polonius.

POLONIUS Well be with you, gentlemen.

HAMLET Hark you, Guildenstern – and you too – at each
 ear a hearer. That great baby you see there is not yet out
 of his swaddling clouts.   374

ROSENCRANTZ Happily he is the second time come to   375
 them, for they say an old man is twice a child.

HAMLET I will prophesy he comes to tell me of the
 players. Mark it. – You say right, sir; a Monday morning, 'twas then indeed.

---

354 *load* i.e. the whole world (with a topical reference to the sign of the
Globe Theatre, a representation of Hercules bearing the world on his
shoulders) 356 *mows* grimaces 358 *'Sblood* by God's blood 364 *garb*
fashion; *extent* showing of welcome 370 *hawk* mattock or pickaxe (also
called 'hack'; here used apparently with a play on 'hawk': a bird); *handsaw*
carpenter's tool (apparently with a play on some corrupt form of 'hern-
shaw'; heron, a bird often hunted with the hawk) 374 *clouts* clothes 375
Happily haply, perhaps

POLONIUS　My lord, I have news to tell you.

381 HAMLET　My lord, I have news to tell you. When Roscius
　　was an actor in Rome –

POLONIUS　The actors are come hither, my lord.

HAMLET　Buzz, buzz.

POLONIUS　Upon my honor –

HAMLET　Then came each actor on his ass –

POLONIUS　The best actors in the world, either for trag-
　　edy, comedy, history, pastoral, pastoral-comical, his-
　　torical-pastoral, tragical-historical, tragical-comical-
390　　historical-pastoral ; scene individable, or poem unlimi-
391　　ted. Seneca cannot be too heavy, nor Plautus too light.
392　　For the law of writ and the liberty, these are the only men.

393 HAMLET　O Jephthah, judge of Israel, what a treasure
　　hadst thou !

POLONIUS　What treasure had he, my lord ?

HAMLET　Why,
　　　　　'One fair daughter, and no more,
398　　　　　　The which he lovèd passing well.'

POLONIUS [aside]　Still on my daughter.

HAMLET　Am I not i' th' right, old Jephthah ?

POLONIUS　If you call me Jephthah, my lord, I have a
　　daughter that I love passing well.

HAMLET　Nay, that follows not.

POLONIUS　What follows then, my lord ?

HAMLET　Why,
　　　　　'As by lot, God wot,'
　　and then, you know,
　　　　　'It came to pass, as most like it was.'

409　　The first row of the pious chanson will show you more,

---

381 *Roscius* the greatest of Roman comic actors　390 *scene individable* drama
observing the unities; *poem unlimited* drama not observing the unities　391
Seneca Roman writer of tragedies; *Plautus* Roman writer of comedies　392
law of writ orthodoxy determined by critical rules of the drama; *liberty* free-
dom from such orthodoxy　393 *Jephthah* the compelled sacrificer of a dearly
beloved daughter (Judges xi)　398 *passing* surpassingly (verses are from a
ballad on Jephthah)　409 *row* stanza; *chanson* song

for look where my abridgment comes.   410
    Enter the Players.
You are welcome, masters, welcome, all. – I am glad to
see thee well. – Welcome, good friends. – O, old friend,
why, thy face is valanced since I saw thee last. Com'st   413
thou to beard me in Denmark? – What, my young lady   414
and mistress? By'r Lady, your ladyship is nearer to
heaven than when I saw you last by the altitude of a
chopine. Pray God your voice, like a piece of uncurrent   417
gold, be not cracked within the ring. – Masters, you are   418
all welcome. We'll e'en to't like French falconers, fly at
anything we see. We'll have a speech straight. Come,
give us a taste of your quality. Come, a passionate speech.

PLAYER What speech, my good lord?

HAMLET I heard thee speak me a speech once, but it was
never acted, or if it was, not above once, for the play, I
remember, pleased not the million; 'twas caviary to the   425
general, but it was (as I received it, and others, whose   426
judgments in such matters cried in the top of mine) an   427
excellent play, well digested in the scenes, set down with
as much modesty as cunning. I remember one said there
were no sallets in the lines to make the matter savory,   430
nor no matter in the phrase that might indict the author
of affectation, but called it an honest method, as wholesome as sweet, and by very much more handsome than
fine. One speech in't I chiefly loved. 'Twas Aeneas' tale
to Dido, and thereabout of it especially where he speaks
of Priam's slaughter. If it live in your memory, begin at   436
this line – let me see, let me see:
    'The rugged Pyrrhus, like th' Hyrcanian beast –'   438

410 *my abridgment* that which shortens my talk   413 *valanced* fringed (with
a beard)   414 *young lady* boy who plays women's parts   417 *chopine*
women's thick-soled shoe; *uncurrent* not legal tender   418 *within the ring*
from the edge through the line circling the design on the coin (with a play
on 'ring': a sound)   425 *caviary* caviare   426 *general* multitude   427 *in the
top of* more authoritatively than   430 *sallets* salads, highly seasoned passages   436 *Priam's slaughter* i.e. at the fall of Troy (Aeneid II, 506 ff.)   438
Hyrcanian beast tiger

'Tis not so ; it begins with Pyrrhus :

440 'The rugged Pyrrhus, he whose sable arms,
  Black as his purpose, did the night resemble
442 When he lay couchèd in the ominous horse,
  Hath now this dread and black complexion smeared
444 With heraldry more dismal. Head to foot
445 Now is he total gules, horridly tricked
  With blood of fathers, mothers, daughters, sons,
447 Baked and impasted with the parching streets,
  That lend a tyrannous and a damnèd light
  To their lord's murder. Roasted in wrath and fire,
450 And thus o'ersizèd with coagulate gore,
  With eyes like carbuncles, the hellish Pyrrhus
  Old grandsire Priam seeks.'
So, proceed you.

POLONIUS Fore God, my lord, well spoken, with good accent and good discretion.

PLAYER   'Anon he finds him,
  Striking too short at Greeks. His antique sword,
  Rebellious to his arms, lies where it falls,
  Repugnant to command. Unequal matched,
  Pyrrhus at Priam drives, in rage strikes wide,
461 But with the whiff and wind of his fell sword
462 Th' unnervèd father falls. Then senseless Ilium,
  Seeming to feel this blow, with flaming top
464 Stoops to his base, and with a hideous crash
  Takes prisoner Pyrrhus' ear. For lo ! his sword,
  Which was declining on the milky head
  Of reverend Priam, seemed i' th' air to stick.
468 So as a painted tyrant Pyrrhus stood,

---

440 *sable* black **442** *ominous* fateful; *horse* the wooden horse by which the Greeks gained entrance to Troy **444** *dismal* ill-omened **445** *gules* red (heraldic term); *tricked* decorated in color (heraldic term) **447** *parching* i.e. because Troy was burning **450** *o'ersizèd* covered as with size, a glutinous material used for filling pores of plaster, etc.; *coagulate* clotted **461** *fell* cruel **462** *senseless* without feeling **464** *his* its **468** *painted* pictured

And like a neutral to his will and matter   469
Did nothing.
But as we often see, against some storm,   471
A silence in the heavens, the rack stand still,   472
The bold winds speechless, and the orb below
As hush as death, anon the dreadful thunder
Doth rend the region, so after Pyrrhus' pause,   475
Aroused vengeance sets him new awork,
And never did the Cyclops' hammers fall   477
On Mars' armor, forged for proof eterne,   478
With less remorse than Pyrrhus' bleeding sword
Now falls on Priam.
Out, out, thou strumpet Fortune! All you gods,
In general synod take away her power,
Break all the spokes and fellies from her wheel,   483
And bowl the round nave down the hill of heaven,   484
As low as to the fiends.'

POLONIUS This is too long.

HAMLET It shall to the barber's, with your beard. –
Prithee say on. He's for a jig or a tale of bawdry, or he   488
sleeps. Say on; come to Hecuba.

PLAYER
'But who (ah woe!) had seen the mobled queen –'   490

HAMLET 'The mobled queen'?

POLONIUS That's good. 'Mobled queen' is good.

PLAYER
'Run barefoot up and down, threat'ning the flames
With bisson rheum; a clout upon that head   494
Where late the diadem stood, and for a robe,
About her lank and all o'erteemèd loins,   496
A blanket in the alarm of fear caught up –

469 *will and matter* purpose and its realization (between which he stands
motionless)   471 *against* just before   472 *rack* clouds   475 *region* sky
477 *Cyclops* giant workmen who made armor in the smithy of Vulcan   478
proof eterne eternal protection   483 *fellies* segments of the rim   484 *nave*
hub   488 *jig* short comic piece with singing and dancing often presented
after a play   490 *mobled* muffled   494 *bisson rheum* blinding tears; *clout*
cloth   496 *o'erteemèd* overproductive of children

Who this had seen, with tongue in venom steeped
499 'Gainst Fortune's state would treason have pro-
nounced.
But if the gods themselves did see her then,
When she saw Pyrrhus make malicious sport
In mincing with his sword her husband's limbs,
The instant burst of clamor that she made
(Unless things mortal move them not at all)
505 Would have made milch the burning eyes of heaven
And passion in the gods.'

507 POLONIUS Look, whe'r he has not turned his color, and
has tears in's eyes. Prithee no more.

HAMLET 'Tis well. I'll have thee speak out the rest of this
510 soon. – Good my lord, will you see the players well bestowed? Do you hear? Let them be well used, for they
are the abstract and brief chronicles of the time. After
your death you were better have a bad epitaph than their
ill report while you live.

POLONIUS My lord, I will use them according to their
desert.

516 HAMLET God's bodkin, man, much better! Use every
man after his desert, and who shall scape whipping?
Use them after your own honor and dignity. The less
they deserve, the more merit is in your bounty. Take
them in.

POLONIUS Come, sirs.

HAMLET Follow him, friends. We'll hear a play to-
morrow. *[aside to Player]* Dost thou hear me, old
friend? Can you play 'The Murder of Gonzago'?

PLAYER Ay, my lord.

HAMLET We'll ha't to-morrow night. You could for a
need study a speech of some dozen or sixteen lines
which I would set down and insert in't, could you not?

PLAYER Ay, my lord.

---

499 *state* government of worldly events   505 *milch* tearful (milk-giving);
eyes i.e. stars   507 *whe'r* whether   510 *bestowed* lodged   516 *God's bodkin*
by God's little body

HAMLET Very well. Follow that lord, and look you mock
   him not. – My good friends, I'll leave you till night. You *530*
   are welcome to Elsinore.   *Exeunt Polonius and Players.*
ROSENCRANTZ Good my lord.
              Exeunt [Rosencrantz and Guildenstern].
HAMLET
   Ay, so, God bye to you. – Now I am alone.
   O, what a rogue and peasant slave am I !
   Is it not monstrous that this player here,
   But in a fiction, in a dream of passion,
   Could force his soul so to his own conceit   *537*
   That from her working all his visage wanned,
   Tears in his eyes, distraction in his aspect,
   A broken voice, and his whole function suiting   *540*
   With forms to his conceit ? And all for nothing,
   For Hecuba !
   What's Hecuba to him, or he to Hecuba,
   That he should weep for her ? What would he do
   Had he the motive and the cue for passion
   That I have ? He would drown the stage with tears
   And cleave the general ear with horrid speech,
   Make mad the guilty and appal the free,
   Confound the ignorant, and amaze indeed
   The very faculties of eyes and ears.
   Yet I,
   A dull and muddy-mettled rascal, peak   *552*
   Like John-a-dreams, unpregnant of my cause,   *553*
   And can say nothing. No, not for a king,
   Upon whose property and most dear life
   A damned defeat was made. Am I a coward ?
   Who calls me villain ? breaks my pate across ?
   Plucks off my beard and blows it in my face ?
   Tweaks me by the nose ? gives me the lie i' th' throat
   As deep as to the lungs ? Who does me this ?

---

537 *conceit* conception, idea   **540** *function* action of bodily powers   **552**
muddy-mettled dull-spirited; *peak* mope   **553** *John-a-dreams* a sleepy
dawdler; *unpregnant* barren of realization

561   Ha, 'swounds, I should take it, for it cannot be
562   But I am pigeon-livered and lack gall
       To make oppression bitter, or ere this
564   I should ha' fatted all the region kites
565   With this slave's offal. Bloody, bawdy villain!
566   Remorseless, treacherous, lecherous, kindless villain!
       O, vengeance!
       Why, what an ass am I! This is most brave,
       That I, the son of a dear father murdered,
       Prompted to my revenge by heaven and hell,
       Must like a whore unpack my heart with words
       And fall a-cursing like a very drab,
573   A stallion! Fie upon't, foh! About, my brains.
       Hum —
       I have heard that guilty creatures sitting at a play
       Have by the very cunning of the scene
577   Been struck so to the soul that presently
       They have proclaimed their malefactions.
       For murder, though it have no tongue, will speak
       With most miraculous organ. I'll have these players
       Play something like the murder of my father
       Before mine uncle. I'll observe his looks.
583   I'll tent him to the quick. If 'a do blench,
       I know my course. The spirit that I have seen
       May be a devil, and the devil hath power
       T' assume a pleasing shape, yea, and perhaps
       Out of my weakness and my melancholy,
       As he is very potent with such spirits,
589   Abuses me to damn me. I'll have grounds
590   More relative than this. The play's the thing
       Wherein I'll catch the conscience of the king.   *Exit.*

*

561 *'swounds* by God's wounds   562 *pigeon-livered* of dove-like gentleness
564 *region kites* kites of the air   565 *offal* guts   566 *kindless* unnatural   573
stallion prostitute (male or female)   577 *presently* immediately   583 *tent*
probe; *blench* flinch   589 *Abuses* deludes   590 *relative* pertinent

Enter King, Queen, Polonius, Ophelia, Rosencrantz, III, i
Guildenstern, Lords.

KING

And can you by no drift of conference   1
Get from him why he puts on this confusion,
Grating so harshly all his days of quiet
With turbulent and dangerous lunacy?

ROSENCRANTZ

He does confess he feels himself distracted,
But from what cause 'a will by no means speak.

GUILDENSTERN

Nor do we find him forward to be sounded,
But with a crafty madness keeps aloof
When we would bring him on to some confession
Of his true state.

QUEEN   Did he receive you well?

ROSENCRANTZ

Most like a gentleman.

GUILDENSTERN

But with much forcing of his disposition.

ROSENCRANTZ

Niggard of question, but of our demands
Most free in his reply.

QUEEN   Did you assay him   14
To any pastime?

ROSENCRANTZ

Madam, it so fell out that certain players
We o'erraught on the way. Of these we told him,   17
And there did seem in him a kind of joy
To hear of it. They are here about the court,
And, as I think, they have already order
This night to play before him.

POLONIUS   'Tis most true,
And he beseeched me to entreat your majesties

III, i A chamber in the Castle   1 *drift of conference* direction of conversation
14 *assay* try to win   17 *o'erraught* overtook

To hear and see the matter.

KING

With all my heart, and it doth much content me
To hear him so inclined.

26 Good gentlemen, give him a further edge
And drive his purpose into these delights.

ROSENCRANTZ

We shall, my lord. *Exeunt Rosencrantz and Guildenstern.*

KING Sweet Gertrude, leave us too,

29 For we have closely sent for Hamlet hither,
That he, as 'twere by accident, may here
31 Affront Ophelia.
32 Her father and myself (lawful espials)
Will so bestow ourselves that, seeing unseen,
We may of their encounter frankly judge
And gather by him, as he is behaved,
If't be th' affliction of his love or no
That thus he suffers for.

QUEEN I shall obey you. –
And for your part, Ophelia, I do wish
That your good beauties be the happy cause
Of Hamlet's wildness. So shall I hope your virtues
Will bring him to his wonted way again,
To both your honors.

OPHELIA Madam, I wish it may. *[Exit Queen.]*

POLONIUS

Ophelia, walk you here. – Gracious, so please you,
We will bestow ourselves. –
   [To Ophelia] Read on this book,
45 That show of such an exercise may color
Your loneliness. We are oft to blame in this,
'Tis too much proved, that with devotion's visage
And pious action we do sugar o'er
The devil himself.

---

26 *edge* keenness of desire 29 *closely* privately 31 *Affront* come face to face
with 32 *espials* spies 45 *exercise* religious exercise (the book being
obviously one of devotion); *color* give an appearance of naturalness to

KING *[aside]*　　　O, 'tis too true.
How smart a lash that speech doth give my conscience!
The harlot's cheek, beautied with plast'ring art,
Is not more ugly to the thing that helps it　　　52
Than is my deed to my most painted word.
O heavy burthen!

POLONIUS
I hear him coming. Let's withdraw, my lord.
　　　　　　　　　[Exeunt King and Polonius.]
　　　Enter Hamlet.

HAMLET
To be, or not to be – that is the question:
Whether 'tis nobler in the mind to suffer
The slings and arrows of outrageous fortune
Or to take arms against a sea of troubles
And by opposing end them. To die, to sleep –
No more – and by a sleep to say we end
The heartache, and the thousand natural shocks
That flesh is heir to. 'Tis a consummation
Devoutly to be wished. To die, to sleep –
To sleep – perchance to dream: ay, there's the rub,　　　65
For in that sleep of death what dreams may come
When we have shuffled off this mortal coil,　　　67
Must give us pause. There's the respect　　　68
That makes calamity of so long life.　　　69
For who would bear the whips and scorns of time,
Th' oppressor's wrong, the proud man's contumely
The pangs of despised love, the law's delay,
The insolence of office, and the spurns
That patient merit of th' unworthy takes,
When he himself might his quietus make　　　75
With a bare bodkin? Who would fardels bear,　　　76

---

52 *to* compared to　65 *rub* obstacle (literally, obstruction encountered by a bowler's ball)　67 *shuffled off* cast off as an encumbrance; *coil* to-do, turmoil　68 *respect* consideration　69 *of so long life* so long-lived　75 *quietus* settlement (literally, release from debt)　76 *bodkin* dagger; *fardels* burdens

To grunt and sweat under a weary life,
But that the dread of something after death,
79   The undiscovered country, from whose bourn
No traveller returns, puzzles the will,
And makes us rather bear those ills we have
Than fly to others that we know not of?
Thus conscience does make cowards of us all,
And thus the native hue of resolution
Is sicklied o'er with the pale cast of thought,
86   And enterprises of great pitch and moment
87   With this regard their currents turn awry
And lose the name of action. – Soft you now,
89   The fair Ophelia! – Nymph, in thy orisons
Be all my sins remembered.

OPHELIA   Good my lord,
How does your honor for this many a day?

HAMLET
I humbly thank you, well, well, well.

OPHELIA
My lord, I have remembrances of yours
That I have longèd long to re-deliver.
I pray you, now receive them.

HAMLET   No, not I,
I never gave you aught.

OPHELIA
My honored lord, you know right well you did,
And with them words of so sweet breath composed
As made the things more rich. Their perfume lost,
Take these again, for to the noble mind
Rich gifts wax poor when givers prove unkind.
There, my lord.

103 HAMLET Ha, ha! Are you honest?
OPHELIA My lord?
HAMLET Are you fair?

79 *bourn* confine, region 86 *pitch* height (of a soaring falcon's flight) 87 *regard* consideration 89 *orisons* prayers (because of the book of devotion she reads) 103 *honest* chaste

OPHELIA What means your lordship?

HAMLET That if you be honest and fair, your honesty
should admit no discourse to your beauty.

OPHELIA Could beauty, my lord, have better commerce 109
than with honesty?

HAMLET Ay, truly; for the power of beauty will sooner
transform honesty from what it is to a bawd than the
force of honesty can translate beauty into his likeness.
This was sometime a paradox, but now the time gives it 114
proof. I did love you once.

OPHELIA Indeed, my lord, you made me believe so.

HAMLET You should not have believed me, for virtue
cannot so inoculate our old stock but we shall relish of it. 118
I loved you not.

OPHELIA I was the more deceived.

HAMLET Get thee to a nunnery. Why wouldst thou be a
breeder of sinners? I am myself indifferent honest, but 122
yet I could accuse me of such things that it were better
my mother had not borne me: I am very proud,
revengeful, ambitious, with more offenses at my beck
than I have thoughts to put them in, imagination to give
them shape, or time to act them in. What should such
fellows as I do crawling between earth and heaven? We
are arrant knaves all; believe none of us. Go thy ways to
a nunnery. Where's your father?

OPHELIA At home, my lord.

HAMLET Let the doors be shut upon him, that he may
play the fool nowhere but in's own house. Farewell.

OPHELIA O, help him, you sweet heavens!

HAMLET If thou dost marry, I'll give thee this plague for
thy dowry: be thou as chaste as ice, as pure as snow, thou
shalt not escape calumny. Get thee to a nunnery. Go,
farewell. Or if thou wilt needs marry, marry a fool, for

109 *commerce* intercourse 114 *paradox* idea contrary to common opinion
118 *inoculate* graft; *relish* have a flavor (because of original sin) 122 *indifferent honest* moderately respectable

139   wise men know well enough what monsters you make
of them. To a nunnery, go, and quickly too. Farewell.

OPHELIA O heavenly powers, restore him!

HAMLET I have heard of your paintings too, well enough.
God hath given you one face, and you make yourselves
another. You jig, you amble, and you lisp; you nickname
145   God's creatures and make your wantonness your ignorance. Go to, I'll no more on't; it hath made me mad.
I say we will have no more marriage. Those that are
married already – all but one – shall live. The rest shall
keep as they are. To a nunnery, go.   *Exit.*

OPHELIA

O, what a noble mind is here o'erthrown!
The courtier's, soldier's, scholar's, eye, tongue, sword,
152   Th' expectancy and rose of the fair state,
153   The glass of fashion and the mould of form,
Th' observed of all observers, quite, quite down!
And I, of ladies most deject and wretched,
That sucked the honey of his music vows,
Now see that noble and most sovereign reason
Like sweet bells jangled, out of time and harsh,
That unmatched form and feature of blown youth
160   Blasted with ecstasy. O, woe is me
T' have seen what I have seen, see what I see!
      Enter King and Polonius.

KING

162   Love? his affections do not that way tend,
Nor what he spake, though it lacked form a little,
Was not like madness. There's something in his soul
O'er which his melancholy sits on brood,
166   And I do doubt the hatch and the disclose
Will be some danger; which for to prevent,

---

139 *monsters* i.e. unnatural combinations of wisdom and uxorious folly   145
wantonness affectation; *your ignorance* a matter for which you offer the excuse
that you don't know any better   152 *expectancy and rose* fair hope   153 *glass*
mirror   160 *ecstasy* madness   162 *affections* emotions   166 *doubt* fear

I have in quick determination
Thus set it down : he shall with speed to England
For the demand of our neglected tribute.
Haply the seas, and countries different,
With variable objects, shall expel
This something-settled matter in his heart,   173
Whereon his brains still beating puts him thus
From fashion of himself. What think you on't ?

POLONIUS
It shall do well. But yet do I believe
The origin and commencement of his grief
Sprung from neglected love. – How now, Ophelia ?
You need not tell us what Lord Hamlet said.
We heard it all. – My lord, do as you please,
But if you hold it fit, after the play
Let his queen mother all alone entreat him
To show his grief. Let her be round with him,   183
And I'll be placed, so please you, in the ear
Of all their conference. If she find him not,
To England send him, or confine him where
Your wisdom best shall think.

KING   It shall be so.
Madness in great ones must not unwatched go. *Exeunt*.

*

Enter Hamlet and three of the Players.   III, ii
HAMLET Speak the speech, I pray you, as I pronounced it
to you, trippingly on the tongue. But if you mouth it, as 2
many of our players do, I had as lief the town crier spoke
my lines. Nor do not saw the air too much with your
hand, thus, but use all gently, for in the very torrent,
tempest, and (as I may say) whirlwind of your passion,
you must acquire and beget a temperance that may give

---

173 *something-settled* somewhat settled   183 *round* plain-spoken
III, ii The hall of the Castle   2 *trippingly* easily

8   it smoothness. O, it offends me to the soul to hear a ro-
9   bustious periwig-pated fellow tear a passion to tatters,
10   to very rags, to split the ears of the groundlings, who for
     the most part are capable of nothing but inexplicable
12   dumb shows and noise. I would have such a fellow
13   whipped for o'erdoing Termagant. It out-herods Herod.
     Pray you avoid it.

PLAYER I warrant your honor.

HAMLET Be not too tame neither, but let your own dis-
     cretion be your tutor. Suit the action to the word, the
     word to the action, with this special observance, that you
     o'erstep not the modesty of nature. For anything so over-
19   done is from the purpose of playing, whose end, both at
     the first and now, was and is, to hold, as 'twere, the mirror
     up to nature, to show virtue her own feature, scorn her
     own image, and the very age and body of the time his
23   form and pressure. Now this overdone, or come tardy off,
     though it make the unskillful laugh, cannot but make
25   the judicious grieve, the censure of the which one must
     in your allowance o'erweigh a whole theatre of others.
     O, there be players that I have seen play, and heard others
     praise, and that highly (not to speak it profanely), that
     neither having th' accent of Christians, nor the gait of
     Christian, pagan, nor man, have so strutted and bellowed
31   that I have thought some of Nature's journeymen had
     made men, and not made them well, they imitated hu-
     manity so abominably.

34 PLAYER I hope we have reformed that indifferently with
     us, sir.

8 *robustious* boisterous 9 *periwig-pated* wig-wearing (after the custom of actors) 10 *groundlings* spectators who paid least and stood on the ground in the pit or yard of the theatre 12 *dumb shows* brief actions without words, forecasting dramatic matter to follow (the play presented later in this scene giving an old-fashioned example) 13 *Termagant* a Saracen 'god' in medieval romance and drama; *Herod* the raging tyrant of old Biblical plays 19 *from* apart from 23 *pressure* impressed or printed character; *come tardy off* brought off slowly and badly 25 *the censure of the which one* the judgment of even one of whom 31 *journeymen* workmen not yet masters of their trade 34 *indifferently* fairly well

94

HAMLET O, reform it altogether! And let those that play
your clowns speak no more than is set down for them, for
there be of them that will themselves laugh, to set on 38
some quantity of barren spectators to laugh too, though
in the mean time some necessary question of the play be
then to be considered. That's villainous and shows a
most pitiful ambition in the fool that uses it. Go make
you ready.　　　　　　　　　　　　*[Exeunt Players.]*

　　Enter Polonius, Guildenstern, and Rosencrantz.

How now, my lord? Will the king hear this piece of
work?

POLONIUS And the queen too, and that presently. 45

HAMLET Bid the players make haste.　　*[Exit Polonius.]*
Will you two help to hasten them?

ROSENCRANTZ Ay, my lord.　　　　　　*Exeunt they two.*

HAMLET What, ho, Horatio!

　　Enter Horatio.

HORATIO

Here, sweet lord, at your service.

HAMLET

Horatio, thou art e'en as just a man
As e'er my conversation coped withal. 52

HORATIO

O, my dear lord –

HAMLET　　　　　　Nay, do not think I flatter.
For what advancement may I hope from thee,
That no revenue hast but thy good spirits
To feed and clothe thee? Why should the poor be
　flattered?
No, let the candied tongue lick absurd pomp,
And crook the pregnant hinges of the knee 58
Where thrift may follow fawning. Dost thou hear? 59
Since my dear soul was mistress of her choice

---

38 *of them* some of them　**45** *presently* at once　**52** *conversation coped withal*
intercourse with men encountered　**58** *pregnant* quick to move　**59** *thrift*
profit

And could of men distinguish her election,
62 S' hath sealed thee for herself, for thou hast been
As one in suff'ring all that suffers nothing,
A man that Fortune's buffets and rewards
Hast ta'en with equal thanks; and blest are those
66 Whose blood and judgment are so well commeddled
That they are not a pipe for Fortune's finger
To sound what stop she please. Give me that man
That is not passion's slave, and I will wear him
In my heart's core, ay, in my heart of heart,
As I do thee. Something too much of this –
There is a play to-night before the king.
One scene of it comes near the circumstance
Which I have told thee, of my father's death.
I prithee, when thou seest that act afoot,
76 Even with the very comment of thy soul
77 Observe my uncle. If his occulted guilt
Do not itself unkennel in one speech,
79 It is a damnèd ghost that we have seen,
And my imaginations are as foul
81 As Vulcan's stithy. Give him heedful note,
For I mine eyes will rivet to his face,
And after we will both our judgments join
84 In censure of his seeming.

HORATIO   Well, my lord.
If 'a steal aught the while this play is playing,
And scape detecting, I will pay the theft.

*Enter Trumpets and Kettledrums, King, Queen,
Polonius, Ophelia [, Rosencrantz, Guildenstern, and
other Lords attendant].*

87 HAMLET They are coming to the play. I must be idle.
Get you a place.

89 KING How fares our cousin Hamlet?

---

62 *sealed* marked   66 *blood* passion; *commeddled* mixed together   76 *the very . . . soul* thy deepest sagacity   77 *occulted* hidden   79 *damnèd ghost* evil spirit, devil (as thought of in II, ii, 584 ff.)   81 *stithy* smithy   84 *censure of* sentence upon   87 *be idle* be foolish, act the madman   89 *cousin* nephew

HAMLET Excellent, i' faith, of the chameleon's dish. I eat 90
the air, promise-crammed. You cannot feed capons so.

KING I have nothing with this answer, Hamlet. These
words are not mine. 93

HAMLET No, nor mine now. *[to Polonius]* My lord, you
played once i' th' university, you say?

POLONIUS That did I, my lord, and was accounted a
good actor.

HAMLET What did you enact?

POLONIUS I did enact Julius Caesar. I was killed i' th'
Capitol; Brutus killed me.

HAMLET It was a brute part of him to kill so capital a calf
there. Be the players ready?

ROSENCRANTZ Ay, my lord. They stay upon your 103
patience.

QUEEN Come hither, my dear Hamlet, sit by me.

HAMLET No, good mother. Here's metal more attractive.

POLONIUS *[to the King]* O ho! do you mark that?

HAMLET Lady, shall I lie in your lap?
    [He lies at Ophelia's feet.]

OPHELIA No, my lord.

HAMLET I mean, my head upon your lap?

OPHELIA Ay, my lord.

HAMLET Do you think I meant country matters? 111

OPHELIA I think nothing, my lord.

HAMLET That's a fair thought to lie between maids' legs.

OPHELIA What is, my lord?

HAMLET Nothing.

OPHELIA You are merry, my lord.

HAMLET Who, I?

OPHELIA Ay, my lord.

HAMLET O God, your only jig-maker! What should a 119

90 *chameleon's dish* i.e. air (which was believed the chameleon's food;
Hamlet willfully takes *fares* in the sense of 'feeds') 93 *not mine* not for me as
the asker of my question 103–04 *stay upon your patience* await your indul-
gence 111 *country matters* rustic goings-on, barnyard mating (with a play
upon a sexual term) 119 *jig-maker* writer of jigs (see II, ii, 488)

man do but be merry? For look you how cheerfully my
mother looks, and my father died within's two hours.

OPHELIA Nay, 'tis twice two months, my lord.

HAMLET So long? Nay then, let the devil wear black, for
124 I'll have a suit of sables. O heavens! die two months
ago, and not forgotten yet? Then there's hope a great
man's memory may outlive his life half a year. But, by'r
Lady, 'a must build churches then, or else shall 'a
128 suffer not thinking on, with the hobby-horse, whose
epitaph is 'For O, for O, the hobby-horse is forgot!'

The trumpets sound. Dumb show follows:
Enter a King and a Queen [very lovingly], the Queen em-
bracing him, and he her. [She kneels; and makes show of
protestation unto him.] He takes her up, and declines his head
upon her neck. He lies him down upon a bank of flowers. She,
seeing him asleep, leaves him. Anon come in another man:
takes off his crown, kisses it, pours poison in the sleeper's ears,
and leaves him. The Queen returns, finds the King dead,
makes passionate action. The poisoner, with some three or
four, come in again, seem to condole with her. The dead body
is carried away. The poisoner woos the Queen with gifts; she
seems harsh awhile, but in the end accepts love.   [Exeunt.]

OPHELIA What means this, my lord?

131 HAMLET Marry, this is miching mallecho; it means mis-
chief.

OPHELIA Belike this show imports the argument of the
play.

Enter Prologue.

HAMLET We shall know by this fellow. The players cannot keep counsel; they'll tell all.

OPHELIA Will 'a tell us what this show meant?

HAMLET Ay, or any show that you'll show him. Be not

---

124 *sables* black furs (luxurious garb, not for mourning)   **128** *hobby-horse*
traditional figure strapped round the waist of a performer in May games and
morris dances   **131** *miching mallecho* sneaking iniquity

you ashamed to show, he'll not shame to tell you what it means.

OPHELIA You are naught, you are naught. I'll mark the 139 play.

PROLOGUE For us and for our tragedy,
Here stooping to your clemency,
We beg your hearing patiently.   [Exit.]

HAMLET Is this a prologue, or the posy of a ring?   143

OPHELIA 'Tis brief, my lord.

HAMLET As woman's love.

Enter [two Players as] King and Queen.

KING

Full thirty times hath Phoebus' cart gone round   146
Neptune's salt wash and Tellus' orbèd ground,   147
And thirty dozen moons with borrowed sheen   148
About the world have times twelve thirties been,
Since love our hearts, and Hymen did our hands,   150
Unite commutual in most sacred bands.   151

QUEEN

So many journeys may the sun and moon
Make us again count o'er ere love be done!
But woe is me, you are so sick of late,
So far from cheer and from your former state,
That I distrust you. Yet, though I distrust,   156
Discomfort you, my lord, it nothing must.
For women fear too much, even as they love,
And women's fear and love hold quantity,   159
In neither aught, or in extremity.
Now what my love is, proof hath made you know,
And as my love is sized, my fear is so.
Where love is great, the littlest doubts are fear;
Where little fears grow great, great love grows there.

---

139 *naught* indecent **143** *posy* brief motto in rhyme ('poesy'); *ring* finger ring **146** *Phoebus' cart* the sun's chariot **147** *Tellus* Roman goddess of the earth **148** *borrowed* i.e. taken from the sun **150** *Hymen* Greek god of marriage **151** *commutual* mutually **156** *distrust you* fear for you **159** *quantity* proportion

KING

Faith, I must leave thee, love, and shortly too;
166   My operant powers their functions leave to do.
And thou shalt live in this fair world behind,
Honored, beloved, and haply one as kind
For husband shalt thou –

QUEEN   O, confound the rest!
Such love must needs be treason in my breast.
In second husband let me be accurst!
None wed the second but who killed the first.

173 HAMLET *[aside]* That's wormwood.

QUEEN
174   The instances that second marriage move
Are base respects of thrift, but none of love.
A second time I kill my husband dead
When second husband kisses me in bed.

KING

I do believe you think what now you speak,
But what we do determine oft we break.
180   Purpose is but the slave to memory,
181   Of violent birth, but poor validity,
Which now like fruit unripe sticks on the tree,
But fall unshaken when they mellow be.
Most necessary 'tis that we forget
To pay ourselves what to ourselves is debt.
What to ourselves in passion we propose,
The passion ending, doth the purpose lose.
The violence of either grief or joy
189   Their own enactures with themselves destroy.
Where joy most revels, grief doth most lament;
Grief joys, joy grieves, on slender accident.
This world is not for aye, nor 'tis not strange
That even our loves should with our fortunes change,

166 *operant powers* active bodily forces   173 *wormwood* a bitter herb   174 *instances* motives   180 *slave to* i.e. dependent upon for life   181 *validity* strength   189 *enactures* fulfillments

For 'tis a question left us yet to prove,
Whether love lead fortune, or else fortune love.
The great man down, you mark his favorite flies,
The poor advanced makes friends of enemies;
And hitherto doth love on fortune tend,
For who not needs shall never lack a friend,
And who in want a hollow friend doth try,
Directly seasons him his enemy.   201
But, orderly to end where I begun,
Our wills and fates do so contrary run
That our devices still are overthrown;   204
Our thoughts are ours, their ends none of our own.
So think thou wilt no second husband wed,
But die thy thoughts when thy first lord is dead.

QUEEN
Nor earth to me give food, nor heaven light,
Sport and repose lock from me day and night,
To desperation turn my trust and hope,
An anchor's cheer in prison be my scope,   211
Each opposite that blanks the face of joy   212
Meet what I would have well, and it destroy,
Both here and hence pursue me lasting strife,   214
If, once a widow, ever I be wife!

HAMLET If she should break it now!
KING
'Tis deeply sworn. Sweet, leave me here awhile.
My spirits grow dull, and fain I would beguile
The tedious day with sleep.
QUEEN   Sleep rock thy brain,   *[He sleeps.]*
And never come mischance between us twain!   *Exit.*

HAMLET Madam, how like you this play?
QUEEN The lady doth protest too much, methinks.
HAMLET O, but she'll keep her word.

---

201 *seasons him* ripens him into   204 *still* always   211 *anchor's* hermit's
212 *blanks* blanches, makes pale   214 *hence* in the next world

224 KING Have you heard the argument? Is there no offense
in't?

HAMLET No, no, they do but jest, poison in jest; no
offense i' th' world.

KING What do you call the play?

229 HAMLET 'The Mousetrap.' Marry, how? Tropically.
This play is the image of a murder done in Vienna. Gonzago is the duke's name; his wife, Baptista. You shall see
anon. 'Tis a knavish piece of work, but what o' that?

233 Your majesty, and we that have free souls, it touches us

234 not. Let the galled jade winch; our withers are unwrung.
         Enter Lucianus.
This is one Lucianus, nephew to the king.

236 OPHELIA You are as good as a chorus, my lord.

HAMLET I could interpret between you and your love, if I

238 could see the puppets dallying.

OPHELIA You are keen, my lord, you are keen.

HAMLET It would cost you a groaning to take off my edge.

OPHELIA Still better, and worse.

HAMLET So you must take your husbands. – Begin, murderer. Leave thy damnable faces and begin. Come, the
croaking raven doth bellow for revenge.

LUCIANUS

Thoughts black, hands apt, drugs fit, and time agreeing,

246 Confederate season, else no creature seeing,
Thou mixture rank, of midnight weeds collected,

248 With Hecate's ban thrice blasted, thrice infected,
Thy natural magic and dire property
On wholesome life usurps immediately.
         [Pours the poison in his ears.]

---

224 *argument* plot summary **229** *Tropically* in the way of a trope or figure
(with a play on 'trapically') **233** *free* guiltless **234** *galled* sore-backed; *jade*
horse; *winch* wince; *withers* shoulders **236** *chorus* one in a play who ex-
plains the action **238** *puppets* i.e. you and your lover as in a puppet show
246 *Confederate season* the occasion being my ally **248** *Hecate* goddess of
witchcraft and black magic; *ban* curse

HAMLET 'A poisons him i' th' garden for his estate. His name 's Gonzago. The story is extant, and written in very choice Italian. You shall see anon how the murderer gets the love of Gonzago's wife.

OPHELIA The king rises.

HAMLET What, frighted with false fire?   256

QUEEN How fares my lord?

POLONIUS Give o'er the play.

KING Give me some light. Away!

POLONIUS Lights, lights, lights!

Exeunt all but Hamlet and Horatio.

HAMLET Why, let the strucken deer go weep,
    The hart ungallèd play.
    For some must watch, while some must sleep;
    Thus runs the world away.

Would not this, sir, and a forest of feathers – if the rest of 265
my fortunes turn Turk with me – with two Provincial 266
roses on my razed shoes, get me a fellowship in a cry of 267
players, sir?

HORATIO Half a share.

HAMLET A whole one, I.
    For thou dost know, O Damon dear,
    This realm dismantled was
    Of Jove himself; and now reigns here
    A very, very – peacock.

HORATIO You might have rhymed.

HAMLET O good Horatio, I'll take the ghost's word for a thousand pound. Didst perceive?

HORATIO Very well, my lord.

HAMLET Upon the talk of the poisoning?

HORATIO I did very well note him.

HAMLET Aha! Come, some music! Come, the recorders! 281

---

256 *false fire* a firing of a gun charged with powder but no shot, a blank-discharge **265** *feathers* plumes for actors' costumes **266** *turn Turk* turn renegade, like a Christian turning Mohammedan **266–67** *Provincial roses* ribbon rosettes **267** *razed* decorated with cut patterns; *cry* pack **281** *recorders* musical instruments of the flute class

For if the king like not the comedy,
283   Why then, belike he likes it not, perdy.
Come, some music!

Enter Rosencrantz and Guildenstern.

GUILDENSTERN Good my lord, vouchsafe me a word with you.

HAMLET Sir, a whole history.

GUILDENSTERN The king, sir—

HAMLET Ay, sir, what of him?

289 GUILDENSTERN Is in his retirement marvellous distempered.

HAMLET With drink, sir?

291 GUILDENSTERN No, my lord, with choler.

HAMLET Your wisdom should show itself more richer to signify this to the doctor, for for me to put him to his purgation would perhaps plunge him into more choler.

GUILDENSTERN Good my lord, put your discourse into
296 some frame, and start not so wildly from my affair.

HAMLET I am tame, sir; pronounce.

GUILDENSTERN The queen, your mother, in most great affliction of spirit hath sent me to you.

HAMLET You are welcome.

GUILDENSTERN Nay, good my lord, this courtesy is not of the right breed. If it shall please you to make me a wholesome answer, I will do your mother's commandment. If not, your pardon and my return shall be the end of my business.

HAMLET Sir, I cannot.

ROSENCRANTZ What, my lord?

HAMLET Make you a wholesome answer; my wit 's diseased. But, sir, such answer as I can make, you shall command, or rather, as you say, my mother. Therefore no more, but to the matter. My mother, you say—

ROSENCRANTZ Then thus she says: your behavior hath

---

283 *perdy* by God ('*par dieu*') 289 *distempered* out of temper, vexed (twisted by Hamlet into 'deranged') 291 *choler* anger (twisted by Hamlet into 'biliousness') 296 *frame* logical order

struck her into amazement and admiration.   313

HAMLET O wonderful son, that can so stonish a mother!
But is there no sequel at the heels of this mother's
admiration? Impart.

ROSENCRANTZ She desires to speak with you in her closet 317
ere you go to bed.

HAMLET We shall obey, were she ten times our mother.
Have you any further trade with us?

ROSENCRANTZ My lord, you once did love me.

HAMLET And do still, by these pickers and stealers.   322

ROSENCRANTZ Good my lord, what is your cause of distemper? You do surely bar the door upon your own
liberty, if you deny your griefs to your friend.

HAMLET Sir, I lack advancement.

ROSENCRANTZ How can that be, when you have the voice
of the king himself for your succession in Denmark?

HAMLET Ay, sir, but 'while the grass grows' – the proverb 329
is something musty.
            Enter the Player with recorders.

O, the recorders. Let me see one. To withdraw with 331
you – why do you go about to recover the wind of me, as 332
if you would drive me into a toil?   333

GUILDENSTERN O my lord, if my duty be too bold, my
love is too unmannerly.   335

HAMLET I do not well understand that. Will you play
upon this pipe?

GUILDENSTERN My lord, I cannot.

HAMLET I pray you.

GUILDENSTERN Believe me, I cannot.

HAMLET I do beseech you.

GUILDENSTERN I know no touch of it, my lord.

HAMLET It is as easy as lying. Govern these ventages 343

---

313 *admiration* wonder   **317** *closet* private room   **322** *pickers and stealers*
i.e. hands   **329** *while the grass grows* (a proverb, ending: 'the horse starves')
331 *recorders* (see III, ii, 281n.); *withdraw* step aside   **332** *recover the wind*
come up to windward like a hunter   **333** *toil* snare   **335** *is too unmannerly*
leads me beyond the restraint of good manners   **343** *ventages* holes, vents

with your fingers and thumb, give it breath with your mouth, and it will discourse most eloquent music. Look you, these are the stops.

GUILDENSTERN But these cannot I command to any utt'rance of harmony. I have not the skill.

HAMLET Why, look you now, how unworthy a thing you make of me! You would play upon me, you would seem to know my stops, you would pluck out the heart of my mystery, you would sound me from my lowest note to the top of my compass; and there is much music, excellent voice, in this little organ, yet cannot you make it speak. 'Sblood, do you think I am easier to be played on than a pipe? Call me what instrument you will, though
357   you can fret me, you cannot play upon me.

Enter Polonius.

God bless you, sir!

POLONIUS My lord, the queen would speak with you,
360   and presently.

HAMLET Do you see yonder cloud that's almost in shape of a camel?

POLONIUS By th' mass and 'tis, like a camel indeed.

HAMLET Methinks it is like a weasel.

POLONIUS It is backed like a weasel.

HAMLET Or like a whale.

POLONIUS Very like a whale.

368 HAMLET Then I will come to my mother by and by.

369 *[aside]* They fool me to the top of my bent. – I will come by and by.

POLONIUS I will say so.   *[Exit.]*

HAMLET 'By and by' is easily said. Leave me, friends.

[Exeunt all but Hamlet.]

'Tis now the very witching time of night,
When churchyards yawn, and hell itself breathes out

---

357 *fret* irritate (with a play on the fret-fingering of certain stringed musical instruments) **360** *presently* at once **368** *by and by* immediately **369** *bent* (see II, ii, 30n.)

Contagion to this world. Now could I drink hot blood
And do such bitter business as the day
Would quake to look on. Soft, now to my mother.
O heart, lose not thy nature; let not ever
The soul of Nero enter this firm bosom.　　　　379
Let me be cruel, not unnatural;
I will speak daggers to her, but use none.
My tongue and soul in this be hypocrites:
How in my words somever she be shent,　　　　383
To give them seals never, my soul, consent!　　*Exit.* 384

*

Enter King, Rosencrantz, and Guildenstern.　　III, iii

KING

I like him not, nor stands it safe with us
To let his madness range. Therefore prepare you.
I your commission will forthwith dispatch,
And he to England shall along with you.
The terms of our estate may not endure　　　　5
Hazard so near's as doth hourly grow
Out of his brows.　　　　　　　　　　　　　7

GUILDENSTERN　We will ourselves provide.
Most holy and religious fear it is
To keep those many many bodies safe
That live and feed upon your majesty.

ROSENCRANTZ

The single and peculiar life is bound　　　　11
With all the strength and armor of the mind
To keep itself from noyance, but much more　　13
That spirit upon whose weal depends and rests
The lives of many. The cess of majesty　　　　15

379 *Nero* murderer of his mother　383 *shent* reproved　384 *seals* authentications in actions
III, iii A chamber in the Castle　5 *terms* circumstances; *estate* royal position　7 *brows* effronteries (apparently with an implication of knitted brows)
11 *peculiar* individual　13 *noyance* harm　15 *cess* cessation, decease

16   Dies not alone, but like a gulf doth draw
        What's near it with it; or 'tis a massy wheel
        Fixed on the summit of the highest mount,
        To whose huge spokes ten thousand lesser things
        Are mortised and adjoined, which when it falls,
        Each small annexment, petty consequence,
22   Attends the boist'rous ruin. Never alone
        Did the king sigh, but with a general groan.

KING

24   Arm you, I pray you, to this speedy voyage,
        For we will fetters put upon this fear,
        Which now goes too free-footed.

ROSENCRANTZ   We will haste us. *Exeunt Gentlemen.*
              Enter Polonius.

POLONIUS

        My lord, he's going to his mother's closet.
        Behind the arras I'll convey myself
29   To hear the process. I'll warrant she'll tax him home,
        And, as you said, and wisely was it said,
        'Tis meet that some more audience than a mother,
        Since nature makes them partial, should o'erhear
33   The speech, of vantage. Fare you well, my liege.
        I'll call upon you ere you go to bed
        And tell you what I know.

KING   Thanks, dear my lord. *Exit [Polonius].*
        O, my offense is rank, it smells to heaven;
37   It hath the primal eldest curse upon't,
        A brother's murder. Pray can I not,
        Though inclination be as sharp as will.
        My stronger guilt defeats my strong intent,
        And like a man to double business bound
        I stand in pause where I shall first begin,

---

16 *gulf* whirlpool   22 *Attends* joins in (like a royal attendant)   24 *Arm*
prepare   29 *process* proceedings; *tax him home* thrust home in reprimanding
him   33 *of vantage* from an advantageous position   37 *primal eldest curse*
that of Cain, who also murdered a brother

And both neglect. What if this cursèd hand
Were thicker than itself with brother's blood,
Is there not rain enough in the sweet heavens
To wash it white as snow? Whereto serves mercy
But to confront the visage of offense?   47
And what's in prayer but this twofold force,
To be forestallèd ere we come to fall,
Or pardoned being down? Then I'll look up.
My fault is past. But, O, what form of prayer
Can serve my turn? 'Forgive me my foul murder'?
That cannot be, since I am still possessed
Of those effects for which I did the murder,   54
My crown, mine own ambition, and my queen.
May one be pardoned and retain th' offense?
In the corrupted currents of this world
Offense's gilded hand may shove by justice,   58
And oft 'tis seen the wicked prize itself
Buys out the law. But 'tis not so above.
There is no shuffling; there the action lies   61
In his true nature, and we ourselves compelled,
Even to the teeth and forehead of our faults,   63
To give in evidence. What then? What rests?
Try what repentance can. What can it not?
Yet what can it when one cannot repent?
O wretched state! O bosom black as death!
O limèd soul, that struggling to be free   68
Art more engaged! Help, angels! Make assay.   69
Bow, stubborn knees, and, heart with strings of steel,
Be soft as sinews of the new-born babe.
All may be well.
    [He kneels.]

---

47 *offense* sin **54** *effects* things acquired **58** *gilded* gold-laden **61** *shuffling* sharp practice, double-dealing; *action* legal proceeding (in heaven's court) **63** *teeth and forehead* face-to-face recognition **68** *limèd* caught in birdlime, a gluey material spread as a bird-snare **69** *engaged* embedded; *assay* an attempt

Enter Hamlet.

HAMLET

73 Now might I do it pat, now 'a is a-praying,
    And now I'll do't. And so 'a goes to heaven,
    And so am I revenged. That would be scanned.
    A villain kills my father, and for that
    I, his sole son, do this same villain send
    To heaven.
    Why, this is hire and salary, not revenge.
80 'A took my father grossly, full of bread,
81 With all his crimes broad blown, as flush as May;
82 And how his audit stands, who knows save heaven?
    But in our circumstance and course of thought,
    'Tis heavy with him; and am I then revenged,
    To take him in the purging of his soul,
    When he is fit and seasoned for his passage?
    No.
88 Up, sword, and know thou a more horrid hent.
    When he is drunk asleep, or in his rage,
    Or in th' incestuous pleasure of his bed,
    At game a-swearing, or about some act
92 That has no relish of salvation in't –
    Then trip him, that his heels may kick at heaven,
    And that his soul may be as damned and black
    As hell, whereto it goes. My mother stays.
    This physic but prolongs thy sickly days.   *Exit.*

KING [*rises*]
    My words fly up, my thoughts remain below.
    Words without thoughts never to heaven go.   *Exit.*

*

73 *pat* opportunely   80 *grossly* in a state of gross unpreparedness; *bread* i.e.
worldly sense gratification   81 *broad blown* fully blossomed; *flush* vigorous
82 *audit* account   88 *more horrid hent* grasping by me on a more horrid
occasion   92 *relish* flavor

Enter [Queen] Gertrude and Polonius. III, iv

POLONIUS

'A will come straight. Look you lay home to him. 1

Tell him his pranks have been too broad to bear with, 2

And that your grace hath screened and stood between

Much heat and him. I'll silence me even here.

Pray you be round with him. 5

[HAMLET *(within)* Mother, mother, mother!]

QUEEN I'll warrant you; fear me not. Withdraw; I hear
him coming. *[Polonius hides behind the arras.]*

Enter Hamlet.

HAMLET

Now, mother, what's the matter?

QUEEN

Hamlet, thou hast thy father much offended.

HAMLET

Mother, you have my father much offended.

QUEEN

Come, come, you answer with an idle tongue. 12

HAMLET

Go, go, you question with a wicked tongue.

QUEEN

Why, how now, Hamlet?

HAMLET   What's the matter now?

QUEEN

Have you forgot me?

HAMLET   No, by the rood, not so! 15

You are the queen, your husband's brother's wife,

And (would it were not so) you are my mother.

QUEEN

Nay, then I'll set those to you that can speak.

HAMLET

Come, come, and sit you down. You shall not budge.

You go not till I set you up a glass

III, iv The private chamber of the Queen   1 *lay* thrust   2 *broad* unres-
trained   5 *round* plain-spoken   12 *idle* foolish   15 *rood* cross

Where you may see the inmost part of you.

QUEEN

What wilt thou do? Thou wilt not murder me?
Help, ho!

POLONIUS *[behind]* What, ho! help!

HAMLET *[draws]*

How now? a rat? Dead for a ducat, dead!
> *[Makes a pass through the arras and kills Polonius.]*

POLONIUS *[behind]*

O, I am slain!

QUEEN   O me, what hast thou done?

HAMLET

Nay, I know not. Is it the king?

QUEEN

O, what a rash and bloody deed is this!

HAMLET

A bloody deed – almost as bad, good mother,
30   As kill a king, and marry with his brother.

QUEEN

As kill a king?

HAMLET   Ay, lady, it was my word.
> *[Lifts up the arras and sees Polonius.]*

Thou wretched, rash, intruding fool, farewell!
I took thee for thy better. Take thy fortune.
Thou find'st to be too busy is some danger. –
Leave wringing of your hands. Peace, sit you down
And let me wring your heart, for so I shall
If it be made of penetrable stuff,
38   If damnèd custom have not brazed it so
39   That it is proof and bulwark against sense.

QUEEN

What have I done that thou dar'st wag thy tongue
In noise so rude against me?

HAMLET   Such an act
That blurs the grace and blush of modesty,

---

38 *custom* habit; *brazed* hardened like brass   39 *proof* armor; *sense* feeling

Calls virtue hypocrite, takes off the rose
From the fair forehead of an innocent love,
And sets a blister there, makes marriage vows   45
As false as dicers' oaths. O, such a deed
As from the body of contraction plucks   47
The very soul, and sweet religion makes   48
A rhapsody of words! Heaven's face does glow,
And this solidity and compound mass,   50
With heated visage, as against the doom,   51
Is thought-sick at the act.

QUEEN   Ay me, what act,
That roars so loud and thunders in the index?   53

HAMLET
Look here upon this picture, and on this,
The counterfeit presentment of two brothers.   55
See what a grace was seated on this brow:
Hyperion's curls, the front of Jove himself,   57
An eye like Mars, to threaten and command,
A station like the herald Mercury   59
New lighted on a heaven-kissing hill –
A combination and a form indeed
Where every god did seem to set his seal
To give the world assurance of a man.
This was your husband. Look you now what follows.
Here is your husband, like a mildewed ear
Blasting his wholesome brother. Have you eyes?
Could you on this fair mountain leave to feed,
And batten on this moor? Ha! have you eyes?   68
You cannot call it love, for at your age
The heyday in the blood is tame, it's humble,   70

---

45 *blister* brand (of degradation) **47** *contraction* the marriage contract **48** *religion* i.e. sacred marriage vows **50** *compound mass* the earth as compounded of the four elements **51** *against* in expectation of; *doom* Day of Judgment **53** *index* table of contents preceding the body of a book **55** *counterfeit presentment* portrayed representation **57** *Hyperion* the sun god; *front* forehead **59** *station* attitude in standing **68** *batten* feed greedily **70** *heyday* excitement of passion

71   And waits upon the judgment, and what judgment
72   Would step from this to this? Sense sure you have,
73   Else could you not have motion, but sure that sense
74   Is apoplexed, for madness would not err,
75   Nor sense to ecstasy was ne'er so thralled
      But it reserved some quantity of choice
      To serve in such a difference. What devil was't
78   That thus hath cozened you at hoodman-blind?
      Eyes without feeling, feeling without sight,
80   Ears without hands or eyes, smelling sans all,
      Or but a sickly part of one true sense
82   Could not so mope.
      O shame, where is thy blush? Rebellious hell,
84   If thou canst mutine in a matron's bones,
      To flaming youth let virtue be as wax
      And melt in her own fire. Proclaim no shame
87   When the compulsive ardor gives the charge,
      Since frost itself as actively doth burn,
89   And reason panders will.

QUEEN   O Hamlet, speak no more.
      Thou turn'st mine eyes into my very soul,
91   And there I see such black and grainèd spots
92   As will not leave their tinct.

HAMLET   Nay, but to live
93   In the rank sweat of an enseamèd bed,
      Stewed in corruption, honeying and making love
      Over the nasty sty —

QUEEN   O, speak to me no more.
      These words like daggers enter in mine ears.
      No more, sweet Hamlet.

HAMLET   A murderer and a villain,

---

71 *waits upon* yields to   72 *Sense* feeling   73 *motion* desire, impulse   74
apoplexed paralyzed   75 *ecstasy* madness   78 *cozened* cheated; *hoodman-blind* blindman's buff   80 *sans* without   82 *mope* be stupid   84 *mutine* mutiny   87 *compulsive* compelling; *gives the charge* delivers the attack   89 *panders will* acts as procurer for desire   91 *grainèd* dyed in grain   92 *tinct* color   93 *enseamèd* grease-laden

A slave that is not twentieth part the tithe   98
Of your precedent lord, a vice of kings,   99
A cutpurse of the empire and the rule,   100
That from a shelf the precious diadem stole
And put it in his pocket –

QUEEN   No more.   102

    Enter [the] Ghost [in his nightgown].

HAMLET
A king of shreds and patches –
Save me and hover o'er me with your wings,
You heavenly guards? What would your gracious figure?

QUEEN
Alas, he's mad.

HAMLET
Do you not come your tardy son to chide,
That, lapsed in time and passion, lets go by   108
Th' important acting of your dread command?
O, say!

GHOST
Do not forget. This visitation
Is but to whet thy almost blunted purpose.
But look, amazement on thy mother sits.
O, step between her and her fighting soul!
Conceit in weakest bodies strongest works.   115
Speak to her, Hamlet.

HAMLET   How is it with you, lady?

QUEEN
Alas, how is't with you,
That you do bend your eye on vacancy,
And with th' incorporal air do hold discourse?   119
Forth at your eyes your spirits wildly peep,
And as the sleeping soldiers in th' alarm

---

98 *tithe* tenth part   99 *vice* clownish rogue (like the Vice of the morality
plays)   100 *cutpurse* skulking thief   102 s.d. *nightgown* dressing gown
108 *lapsed . . . passion* having let the moment slip and passion cool   115
Conceit imagination   119 *incorporal* bodiless

122 Your bedded hairs like life in excrements
123 Start up and stand an end. O gentle son,
124 Upon the heat and flame of thy distemper
Sprinkle cool patience. Whereon do you look?

HAMLET
On him, on him! Look you, how pale he glares!
His form and cause conjoined, preaching to stones,
128 Would make them capable. – Do not look upon me,
Lest with this piteous action you convert
130 My stern effects. Then what I have to do
Will want true color – tears perchance for blood.

QUEEN
To whom do you speak this?

HAMLET   Do you see nothing there?

QUEEN
Nothing at all; yet all that is I see.

HAMLET
Nor did you nothing hear?

QUEEN   No, nothing but ourselves.

HAMLET
Why, look you there! Look how it steals away!
My father, in his habit as he lived!
Look where he goes even now out at the portal!

                                                      Exit Ghost.

QUEEN
This is the very coinage of your brain.
139 This bodiless creation ecstasy
Is very cunning in.

HAMLET   Ecstasy?
My pulse as yours doth temperately keep time
And makes as healthful music. It is not madness
That I have uttered. Bring me to the test,
And I the matter will reword, which madness

---

122 *excrements* outgrowths 123 *an* on 124 *distemper* mental disorder
128 *capable* susceptible 130 *effects* manifestations of emotion and purpose
139 *ecstasy* madness

Would gambol from. Mother, for love of grace,   145
Lay not that flattering unction to your soul,   146
That not your trespass but my madness speaks.
It will but skin and film the ulcerous place
Whiles rank corruption, mining all within,   149
Infects unseen. Confess yourself to heaven,
Repent what's past, avoid what is to come,
And do not spread the compost on the weeds   152
To make them ranker. Forgive me this my virtue.
For in the fatness of these pursy times   154
Virtue itself of vice must pardon beg,
Yea, curb and woo for leave to do him good.   156

QUEEN
O Hamlet, thou hast cleft my heart in twain.

HAMLET
O, throw away the worser part of it,
And live the purer with the other half.
Good night – but go not to my uncle's bed.
Assume a virtue, if you have it not.
That monster custom, who all sense doth eat,   162
Of habits devil, is angel yet in this,
That to the use of actions fair and good
He likewise gives a frock or livery   165
That aptly is put on. Refrain to-night,
And that shall lend a kind of easiness
To the next abstinence; the next more easy;
For use almost can change the stamp of nature,   169
And either ... the devil, or throw him out   170
With wondrous potency. Once more, good night,
And when you are desirous to be blest,
I'll blessing beg of you. – For this same lord,

145 *gambol* shy (like a startled horse)   146 *unction* ointment   149 *mining* undermining   152 *compost* fertilizing mixture   154 *fatness* gross slackness; *pursy* corpulent   156 *curb* bow to   162–63 *all sense ... devil* (see Appendix: Supplementary Notes)   165 *livery* characteristic dress (accompanying the suggestion of 'garb' in *habits*)   169 *use* habit; *stamp* impression, form   170 *And ... out* (see Appendix: Supplementary Notes)

I do repent; but heaven hath pleased it so,
To punish me with this, and this with me,
That I must be their scourge and minister.

177 I will bestow him and will answer well
The death I gave him. So again, good night.
I must be cruel only to be kind.

180 Thus bad begins, and worse remains behind.
One word more, good lady.

QUEEN   What shall I do?

HAMLET
Not this, by no means, that I bid you do:

183 Let the bloat king tempt you again to bed,
Pinch wanton on your cheek, call you his mouse,

185 And let him, for a pair of reechy kisses,
Or paddling in your neck with his damned fingers,

187 Make you to ravel all this matter out,
That I essentially am not in madness,
But mad in craft. 'Twere good you let him know,
For who that's but a queen, fair, sober, wise,

191 Would from a paddock, from a bat, a gib,

192 Such dear concernings hide? Who would do so?
No, in despite of sense and secrecy,
Unpeg the basket on the house's top,

195 Let the birds fly, and like the famous ape,

196 To try conclusions, in the basket creep
And break your own neck down.

QUEEN
Be thou assured, if words be made of breath,
And breath of life, I have no life to breathe
What thou hast said to me.

HAMLET
I must to England; you know that?

---

177 *bestow* stow, hide   180 *behind* to come   183 *bloat* bloated with sense
gratification   185 *reechy* filthy   187 *ravel . . . out* disentangle   191 *paddock* toad; *gib* tomcat   192 *dear concernings* matters of great personal significance   195 *famous ape* (one in a story now unknown)   196 *conclusions* experiments

QUEEN   Alack,
    I had forgot. 'Tis so concluded on.

HAMLET
    There's letters sealed, and my two schoolfellows,
    Whom I will trust as I will adders fanged,
    They bear the mandate; they must sweep my way   205
    And marshal me to knavery. Let it work.
    For 'tis the sport to have the enginer   207
    Hoist with his own petar, and 't shall go hard   208
    But I will delve one yard below their mines
    And blow them at the moon. O, 'tis most sweet
    When in one line two crafts directly meet.
    This man shall set me packing.   212
    I'll lug the guts into the neighbor room.
    Mother, good night. Indeed, this counsellor
    Is now most still, most secret, and most grave,
    Who was in life a foolish prating knave.
    Come, sir, to draw toward an end with you.
    Good night, mother.
             [Exit the Queen. Then] exit [Hamlet,
                        tugging in Polonius].

*

Enter King and Queen, with Rosencrantz and   IV, i
    Guildenstern.

KING
    There's matter in these sighs. These profound heaves
    You must translate; 'tis fit we understand them.
    Where is your son?

QUEEN
    Bestow this place on us a little while.

---

205 *mandate* order 207 *enginer* engineer, constructor of military engines or
works 208 *Hoist* blown up; *petar* petard, bomb or mine 212 *packing*
travelling in a hurry (with a play upon his 'packing' or shouldering of
Polonius' body and also upon his 'packing' in the sense of 'plotting' or
'contriving')
IV, i A chamber in the Castle

[Exeunt Rosencrantz and Guildenstern.]
Ah, mine own lord, what have I seen to-night!

KING
What, Gertrude? How does Hamlet?

QUEEN
Mad as the sea and wind when both contend
Which is the mightier. In his lawless fit,
Behind the arras hearing something stir,
Whips out his rapier, cries, 'A rat, a rat!'

11   And in this brainish apprehension kills
The unseen good old man.

KING   O heavy deed!
It had been so with us, had we been there.
His liberty is full of threats to all,
To you yourself, to us, to every one.
Alas, how shall this bloody deed be answered?

17   It will be laid to us, whose providence
18   Should have kept short, restrained, and out of haunt
This mad young man. But so much was our love
We would not understand what was most fit,
But, like the owner of a foul disease,

22   To keep it from divulging, let it feed
Even on the pith of life. Where is he gone?

QUEEN
To draw apart the body he hath killed;
25   O'er whom his very madness, like some ore
26   Among a mineral of metals base,
Shows itself pure. 'A weeps for what is done.

KING
O Gertrude, come away!
The sun no sooner shall the mountains touch
But we will ship him hence, and this vile deed
We must with all our majesty and skill
Both countenance and excuse. Ho, Guildenstern!

---

11 *brainish apprehension* headstrong conception   17 *providence* foresight
18 *haunt* association with others   22 *divulging* becoming known   25 *ore*
vein of gold   26 *mineral* mine

Enter Rosencrantz and Guildenstern.
Friends both, go join you with some further aid.
Hamlet in madness hath Polonius slain,
And from his mother's closet hath he dragged him.
Go seek him out; speak fair, and bring the body
Into the chapel. I pray you haste in this.
                    [Exeunt Rosencrantz and Guildenstern.]
Come, Gertrude, we'll call up our wisest friends
And let them know **both** what we mean to do
And what's untimely done . . .   40
Whose whisper o'er the world's diameter,
As level as the cannon to his blank   42
Transports his poisoned shot, may miss our name
And hit the woundless air. O, come away!
My soul is full of discord and dismay.   *Exeunt.*

*

Enter Hamlet.   IV, ii
HAMLET Safely stowed.
GENTLEMEN *(within)* Hamlet! Lord Hamlet!
HAMLET But soft, what noise? Who calls on Hamlet? O,
    here they come.
        [Enter] Rosencrantz, [Guildenstern,] and others.
ROSENCRANTZ
    What have you done, my lord, with the dead body?
HAMLET
    Compounded it with dust, whereto 'tis kin.
ROSENCRANTZ
    Tell us where 'tis, that we may take it thence
    And bear it to the chapel.
HAMLET Do not believe it.
ROSENCRANTZ Believe what?
HAMLET That I can keep your counsel and not mine own.

---

40 *And . . . done* (see Appendix: Supplementary Notes)   42 *As level* with as
direct aim; *blank* mark, central white spot on a target
IV, ii A passage in the Castle

12   Besides, to be demanded of a sponge, what replication
should be made by the son of a king?

ROSENCRANTZ Take you me for a sponge, my lord?

15 HAMLET Ay, sir, that soaks up the king's countenance,
his rewards, his authorities. But such officers do the king
best service in the end. He keeps them, like an ape, in
the corner of his jaw, first mouthed, to be last swal-
lowed. When he needs what you have gleaned, it is but
squeezing you and, sponge, you shall be dry again.

ROSENCRANTZ I understand you not, my lord.

22 HAMLET I am glad of it. A knavish speech sleeps in a
foolish ear.

ROSENCRANTZ My lord, you must tell us where the
body is and go with us to the king.

HAMLET The body is with the king, but the king is not
with the body. The king is a thing –

GUILDENSTERN A thing, my lord?

29 HAMLET Of nothing. Bring me to him. Hide fox, and all
after.   *Exeunt.*

*

IV, iii   *Enter King, and two or three.*

KING

I have sent to seek him and to find the body.
How dangerous is it that this man goes loose!
Yet must not we put the strong law on him;

4 He's loved of the distracted multitude,
Who like not in their judgment, but their eyes,

6 And where 'tis so, th' offender's scourge is weighed,
But never the offense. To bear all smooth and even,

---

12 *replication* reply   15 *countenance* favor   22 *sleeps in* means nothing to
29 *Of nothing* (cf. Prayer Book, Psalm cxliv, 4, 'Man is like a thing of naught:
his time passeth away like a shadow')   29–30 *Hide . . . after* (apparently well-
known words from some game of hide-and-seek)
IV, iii A chamber in the Castle   4 *distracted* confused   6 *scourge* punishment

This sudden sending him away must seem
Deliberate pause. Diseases desperate grown 9
By desperate appliance are relieved,
Or not at all.

   Enter Rosencrantz, [Guildenstern,] and all the rest.
    How now ? What hath befallen ?

ROSENCRANTZ
Where the dead body is bestowed, my lord,
We cannot get from him.

KING   But where is he ?

ROSENCRANTZ
Without, my lord ; guarded, to know your pleasure.

KING
Bring him before us.

ROSENCRANTZ   Ho ! Bring in the lord.
   They enter [with Hamlet].

KING Now, Hamlet, where's Polonius ?

HAMLET At supper.

KING At supper ? Where ?

HAMLET Not where he eats, but where 'a is eaten. A
certain convocation of politic worms are e'en at him. 20
Your worm is your only emperor for diet. We fat 21
all creatures else to fat us, and we fat ourselves for
maggots. Your fat king and your lean beggar is but
variable service – two dishes, but to one table. That's 24
the end.

KING Alas, alas !

HAMLET A man may fish with the worm that hath eat of a
king, and eat of the fish that hath fed of that worm.

KING What dost thou mean by this ?

HAMLET Nothing but to show you how a king may go a

9 *Deliberate pause* something done with much deliberation 20 *politic worms*
political and craftily scheming worms (such as Polonius might well attract)
21 *diet* food and drink (perhaps with a play upon a famous 'convocation,'
the Diet of Worms opened by the Emperor Charles V on January 28, 1521,
before which Luther appeared) 24 *variable service* different servings of one
food

31   progress through the guts of a beggar.

KING Where is Polonius?

HAMLET In heaven. Send thither to see. If your messenger find him not there, seek him i' th' other place yourself. But if indeed you find him not within this month, you shall nose him as you go up the stairs into the lobby.

KING *[to Attendants]* Go seek him there.

HAMLET 'A will stay till you come.   *[Exeunt Attendants.]*

KING

    Hamlet, this deed, for thine especial safety,

40   Which we do tender as we dearly grieve

    For that which thou hast done, must send thee hence

    With fiery quickness. Therefore prepare thyself.

    The bark is ready and the wind at help,

44   Th' associates tend, and everything is bent

    For England.

HAMLET   For England?

KING   Ay, Hamlet.

HAMLET   Good.

KING

    So is it, if thou knew'st our purposes.

47 HAMLET I see a cherub that sees them. But come, for England! Farewell, dear mother.

KING Thy loving father, Hamlet.

HAMLET My mother – father and mother is man and wife, man and wife is one flesh, and so, my mother. Come, for England!   *Exit.*

KING

53   Follow him at foot; tempt him with speed aboard.

    Delay it not; I'll have him hence to-night.

    Away! for everything is sealed and done

56   That else leans on th' affair. Pray you make haste.

              [Exeunt all but the King.]

---

31 *progress* royal journey of state 40 *tender* hold dear; *dearly* intensely 44 *tend* wait; *bent* set in readiness (like a bent bow) 47 *cherub* one of the cherubim (angels with a distinctive quality of knowledge) 53 *at foot* at heel, close 56 *leans on* is connected with

And, England, if my love thou hold'st at aught –   57
As my great power thereof may give thee sense,
Since yet thy cicatrice looks raw and red
After the Danish sword, and thy free awe   60
Pays homage to us – thou mayst not coldly set   61
Our sovereign process, which imports at full   62
By letters congruing to that effect   63
The present death of Hamlet. Do it, England,   64
For like the hectic in my blood he rages,   65
And thou must cure me. Till I know 'tis done,
Howe'er my haps, my joys were ne'er begun.   *Exit.* 67

*

Enter Fortinbras with his Army over the stage.   IV, iv

FORTINBRAS
Go, captain, from me greet the Danish king.
Tell him that by his license Fortinbras
Craves the conveyance of a promised march   3
Over his kingdom. You know the rendezvous.
If that his majesty would aught with us,
We shall express our duty in his eye ;   6
And let him know so.

CAPTAIN   I will do't, my lord.

FORTINBRAS
Go softly on.   *[Exeunt all but the Captain.]* 8
          *Enter Hamlet, Rosencrantz, [Guildenstern,] and
          others.*

HAMLET
Good sir, whose powers are these ?   9

CAPTAIN
They are of Norway, sir.

57 *England* King of England   60 *free awe* voluntary show of respect   61 *set*
esteem   62 *process* formal command   63 *congruing* agreeing   64 *present*
instant   65 *hectic* a continuous fever   67 *haps* fortunes
IV, iv A coastal highway   3 *conveyance* escort   6 *eye* presence   8 *softly*
slowly   9 *powers* forces

HAMLET
How purposed, sir, I pray you?

CAPTAIN
Against some part of Poland.

HAMLET
Who commands them, sir?

CAPTAIN
The nephew to old Norway, Fortinbras.

HAMLET
15   Goes it against the main of Poland, sir,
Or for some frontier?

CAPTAIN
17   Truly to speak, and with no addition,
We go to gain a little patch of ground
That hath in it no profit but the name.
20   To pay five ducats, five, I would not farm it,
Nor will it yield to Norway or the Pole
22   A ranker rate, should it be sold in fee.

HAMLET
Why, then the Polack never will defend it.

CAPTAIN
Yes, it is already garrisoned.

HAMLET
Two thousand souls and twenty thousand ducats
Will not debate the question of this straw.
27   This is th' imposthume of much wealth and peace,
That inward breaks, and shows no cause without
Why the man dies. I humbly thank you, sir.

CAPTAIN
God bye you, sir.   *[Exit.]*

ROSENCRANTZ   Will't please you go, my lord?

HAMLET
I'll be with you straight. Go a little before.
                              [Exeunt all but Hamlet.]

---

15 *main* main body   17 *addition* exaggeration   20 *To pay* i.e. for a yearly
rental of   22 *ranker* more abundant; *in fee* outright   27 *imposthume* abscess

How all occasions do inform against me 32
And spur my dull revenge! What is a man,
If his chief good and market of his time 34
Be but to sleep and feed? A beast, no more.
Sure he that made us with such large discourse, 36
Looking before and after, gave us not
That capability and godlike reason
To fust in us unused. Now, whether it be 39
Bestial oblivion, or some craven scruple 40
Of thinking too precisely on th' event – 41
A thought which, quartered, hath but one part wisdom
And ever three parts coward – I do not know
Why yet I live to say, 'This thing's to do,'
Sith I have cause, and will, and strength, and means
To do't. Examples gross as earth exhort me. 46
Witness this army of such mass and charge, 47
Led by a delicate and tender prince,
Whose spirit, with divine ambition puffed,
Makes mouths at the invisible event, 50
Exposing what is mortal and unsure
To all that fortune, death, and danger dare,
Even for an eggshell. Rightly to be great
Is not to stir without great argument,
But greatly to find quarrel in a straw 55
When honor's at the stake. How stand I then,
That have a father killed, a mother stained,
Excitements of my reason and my blood,
And let all sleep, while to my shame I see
The imminent death of twenty thousand men
That for a fantasy and trick of fame 61
Go to their graves like beds, fight for a plot

---

32 *inform* take shape   34 *market of* compensation for   36 *discourse* power
of thought   39 *fust* grow mouldy   40 *oblivion* forgetfulness   41 *event*
outcome (as also in l. 50)   46 *gross* large and evident   47 *charge* expense
50 *Makes mouths* makes faces scornfully   55 *greatly . . . straw* to recognize
the great argument even in some small matter   61 *fantasy* fanciful image;
trick toy

63   Whereon the numbers cannot try the cause,
64   Which is not tomb enough and continent
     To hide the slain ? O, from this time forth,
     My thoughts be bloody, or be nothing worth !   *Exit.*

*

IV, v   *Enter Horatio, [Queen] Gertrude, and a Gentleman.*

QUEEN
  I will not speak with her.

GENTLEMAN
2   She is importunate, indeed distract.
    Her mood will needs be pitied.

QUEEN   What would she have ?

GENTLEMAN
    She speaks much of her father, says she hears
5   There's tricks i' th' world, and hems, and beats her heart,
6   Spurns enviously at straws, speaks things in doubt
    That carry but half sense. Her speech is nothing,
8   Yet the unshapèd use of it doth move
9   The hearers to collection ; they aim at it,
10 And botch the words up fit to their own thoughts,
    Which, as her winks and nods and gestures yield them,
    Indeed would make one think there might be thought,
    Though nothing sure, yet much unhappily.

HORATIO
  'Twere good she were spoken with, for she may strew
  Dangerous conjectures in ill-breeding minds.

QUEEN
  Let her come in.   *[Exit Gentleman.]*

---

63 *try the cause* find space in which to settle the issue by battle   64 *continent*
receptacle
IV, v A chamber in the Castle   2 *distract* insane   5 *tricks* deceits   6 *Spurns
enviously* kicks spitefully, takes offense; *straws* trifles   8 *unshapèd use*
disordered manner   9 *collection* attempts at shaping meaning; *aim* guess
10 *botch* patch

[Aside]
To my sick soul (as sin's true nature is)
Each toy seems prologue to some great amiss.   18
So full of artless jealousy is guilt   19
It spills itself in fearing to be spilt.   20
    Enter Ophelia [distracted].

OPHELIA
Where is the beauteous majesty of Denmark?
QUEEN How now, Ophelia?
OPHELIA
She sings. How should I your true-love know
           From another one?
      By his cockle hat and staff   25
           And his sandal shoon.   26

QUEEN
Alas, sweet lady, what imports this song?
OPHELIA Say you? Nay, pray you mark.

              Song.

      He is dead and gone, lady,
        He is dead and gone;
      At his head a grass-green turf,
        At his heels a stone.

O, ho!
QUEEN Nay, but Ophelia—
OPHELIA Pray you mark.
  [Sings] White his shroud as the mountain snow—
    Enter King.
QUEEN Alas, look here, my lord.

OPHELIA   *Song.*
      Larded all with sweet flowers;   38

---

18 *toy* trifle; *amiss* calamity   19 *artless* unskillfully managed; *jealousy* suspicion   20 *spills* destroys   25 *cockle hat* hat bearing a cockle shell, worn by a pilgrim who had been to the shrine of St James of Compostela   26 *shoon* shoes   38 *Larded* garnished

> Which bewept to the grave did not go
> With true-love showers.

KING How do you, pretty lady?

42 **OPHELIA** Well, God dild you! They say the owl was a baker's daughter. Lord, we know what we are, but know not what we may be. God be at your table!

45 **KING** Conceit upon her father.

OPHELIA Pray let's have no words of this, but when they ask you what it means, say you this:

Song.

> To-morrow is Saint Valentine's day.
49 > All in the morning betime,
> And I a maid at your window,
> To be your Valentine.
> Then up he rose and donned his clo'es
53 > And dupped the chamber door,
> Let in the maid, that out a maid
> Never departed more.

KING Pretty Ophelia!

OPHELIA Indeed, la, without an oath, I'll make an end on't:

58 *[Sings]* By Gis and by Saint Charity,
> Alack, and fie for shame!
> Young men will do't if they come to't.
61 > By Cock, they are to blame.
> Quoth she, 'Before you tumbled me,
> You promised me to wed.'
He answers:
> 'So would I 'a' done, by yonder sun,
> And thou hadst not come to my bed.'

KING How long hath she been thus?

---

42 *dild* yield, repay; *the owl* an owl into which, according to a folk-tale, a baker's daughter was transformed because of her failure to show whole-hearted generosity when Christ asked for bread in the baker's shop 45 *Conceit* thought 49 *betime* early 53 *dupped* opened 58 *Gis* Jesus 61 *Cock* God (with a perversion of the name not uncommon in oaths)

OPHELIA I hope all will be well. We must be patient, but
    I cannot choose but weep to think they would lay him i'
    th' cold ground. My brother shall know of it; and so I   70
    thank you for your good counsel. Come, my coach!
    Good night, ladies, good night. Sweet ladies, good
    night, good night.   *[Exit.]*

KING
    Follow her close; give her good watch, I pray you.
                                     [Exit Horatio.]
    O, this is the poison of deep grief; it springs
    All from her father's death – and now behold!
    O Gertrude, Gertrude,
    When sorrows come, they come not single spies,
    But in battalions: first, her father slain;
    Next, your son gone, and he most violent author
    Of his own just remove; the people muddied,   81
    Thick and unwholesome in their thoughts and whispers
    For good Polonius' death, and we have done but greenly 83
    In hugger-mugger to inter him; poor Ophelia   84
    Divided from herself and her fair judgment,
    Without the which we are pictures or mere beasts;
    Last, and as much containing as all these,
    Her brother is in secret come from France,
    Feeds on his wonder, keeps himself in clouds,   89
    And wants not buzzers to infect his ear   90
    With pestilent speeches of his father's death,
    Wherein necessity, of matter beggared,   92
    Will nothing stick our person to arraign   93
    In ear and ear. O my dear Gertrude, this,
    Like to a murd'ring piece, in many places   95
    Gives me superfluous death.
        A noise within.

---

81 *muddied* stirred up and confused   83 *greenly* foolishly   84 *hugger-mugger* secrecy and disorder   89 *clouds* obscurity   90 *wants* lacks; *buzzers* whispering tale-bearers   92 *of matter beggared* unprovided with facts   93 *nothing stick* in no way hesitate; *arraign* accuse   95 *murd'ring piece* cannon loaded with shot meant to scatter

Enter a Messenger.

QUEEN   Alack, what noise is this?

KING
97 Attend, where are my Switzers? Let them guard the
    door.
    What is the matter?

MESSENGER   Save yourself, my lord.
99   The ocean, overpeering of his list,
100 Eats not the flats with more impiteous haste
101 Than young Laertes, in a riotous head,
     O'erbears your officers. The rabble call him lord,
     And, as the world were now but to begin,
     Antiquity forgot, custom not known,
105 The ratifiers and props of every word,
     They cry, 'Choose we! Laertes shall be king!'
     Caps, hands, and tongues applaud it to the clouds,
     'Laertes shall be king! Laertes king!'
            A noise within.

QUEEN
     How cheerfully on the false trail they cry!
110 O, this is counter, you false Danish dogs!

KING
     The doors are broke.
            Enter Laertes with others.

LAERTES
     Where is this king? – Sirs, stand you all without.

ALL
     No, let's come in.

LAERTES   I pray you give me leave.

ALL We will, we will.

LAERTES
     I thank you. Keep the door.   *[Exeunt his Followers.]*
                              O thou vile king,
     Give me my father.

97 *Switzers* hired Swiss guards 99 *overpeering of* rising to look over and
pass beyond; *list* boundary 100 *impiteous* pitiless 101 *head* armed force
105 *word* promise 110 *counter* hunting backward on the trail

QUEEN   Calmly, good Laertes.

LAERTES

That drop of blood that's calm proclaims me bastard,
Cries cuckold to my father, brands the harlot
Even here between the chaste unsmirchèd brows
Of my true mother.

KING   What is the cause, Laertes,
That thy rebellion looks so giant-like?
Let him go, Gertrude. Do not fear our person.   122
There's such divinity doth hedge a king
That treason can but peep to what it would,   124
Acts little of his will. Tell me, Laertes,
Why thou art thus incensed. Let him go, Gertrude.
Speak, man.

LAERTES

Where is my father?

KING   Dead.

QUEEN   But not by him.

KING

Let him demand his fill.

LAERTES

How came he dead? I'll not be juggled with.
To hell allegiance, vows to the blackest devil,
Conscience and grace to the profoundest pit!
I dare damnation. To this point I stand,
That both the worlds I give to negligence,   134
Let come what comes, only I'll be revenged
Most throughly for my father.   136

KING   Who shall stay you?

LAERTES

My will, not all the world's.
And for my means, I'll husband them so well
They shall go far with little.

KING   Good Laertes,

122 *fear* fear for   124 *peep to* i.e. through the barrier   134 *both the worlds*
whatever may result in this world or the next; *give to negligence* disregard
136 *throughly* thoroughly

If you desire to know the certainty
Of your dear father, is't writ in your revenge
142   That swoopstake you will draw both friend and foe,
Winner and loser?

LAERTES

None but his enemies.

KING   Will you know them then?

LAERTES

To his good friends thus wide I'll ope my arms
146   And like the kind life-rend'ring pelican
Repast them with my blood.

KING   Why, now you speak
Like a good child and a true gentleman.
That I am guiltless of your father's death,
150   And am most sensibly in grief for it,
151   It shall as level to your judgment 'pear
As day does to your eye.

        A noise within : 'Let her come in.'

LAERTES

How now? What noise is that?

        Enter Ophelia.

O heat, dry up my brains; tears seven times salt
Burn out the sense and virtue of mine eye!
By heaven, thy madness shall be paid by weight
157   Till our scale turn the beam. O rose of May,
Dear maid, kind sister, sweet Ophelia!
O heavens, is't possible a young maid's wits
Should be as mortal as an old man's life?
161   [Nature is fine in love, and where 'tis fine,
162   It sends some precious instance of itself
After the thing it loves.]

142 *swoopstake* sweepstake, taking all stakes on the gambling table   146
life-rend'ring life-yielding (because the mother pelican supposedly took
blood from her breast with her bill to feed her young)   150 *sensibly* feelingly
151 *level* plain   157 *beam* bar of a balance   161 *fine* refined to purity   162
instance token

OPHELIA   *Song.*

> They bore him barefaced on the bier
>   [Hey non nony, nony, hey nony]
>   And in his grave rained many a tear –
> Fare you well, my dove!

LAERTES
Hadst thou thy wits, and didst persuade revenge,
It could not move thus.

OPHELIA You must sing 'A-down a-down, and you call
him a-down-a.' O, how the wheel becomes it! It is the 171
false steward, that stole his master's daughter.

LAERTES This nothing's more than matter.   173

OPHELIA There's rosemary, that's for remembrance.
Pray you, love, remember. And there is pansies, that's
for thoughts.

LAERTES A document in madness, thoughts and re-   177
membrance fitted.

OPHELIA There's fennel for you, and columbines.   179
There's rue for you, and here's some for me. We may   180
call it herb of grace o' Sundays. O, you must wear your
rue with a difference. There's a daisy. I would give you 182
some violets, but they withered all when my father died. 183
They say 'a made a good end.
[Sings] For bonny sweet Robin is all my joy.

LAERTES
Thought and affliction, passion, hell itself,
She turns to favor and to prettiness.   187

OPHELIA   *Song.*

> And will 'a not come again?
> And will 'a not come again?
>   No, no, he is dead;

---

171 *wheel* burden, refrain   173 *more than matter* more meaningful than sane
speech   177 *document* lesson   179 *fennel* symbol of flattery; *columbines*
symbol of·thanklessness (?)   180 *rue* symbol of repentance   182 *daisy*
symbol of dissembling   183 *violets* symbol of faithfulness   187 *favor*
charm

Go to thy deathbed;
He never will come again.
His beard was as white as snow,
194 All flaxen was his poll.
He is gone, he is gone,
And we cast away moan.
God 'a' mercy on his soul!
198 And of all Christian souls, I pray God. God bye you.
[Exit.]

LAERTES
Do you see this, O God?

KING
Laertes, I must commune with your grief,
Or you deny me right. Go but apart,
Make choice of whom your wisest friends you will,
And they shall hear and judge 'twixt you and me.
204 If by direct or by collateral hand
205 They find us touched, we will our kingdom give,
Our crown, our life, and all that we call ours,
To you in satisfaction; but if not,
Be you content to lend your patience to us,
And we shall jointly labor with your soul
To give it due content.

LAERTES   Let this be so.
His means of death, his obscure funeral—
212 No trophy, sword, nor hatchment o'er his bones,
213 No noble rite nor formal ostentation—
Cry to be heard, as 'twere from heaven to earth,
215 That I must call't in question.

KING   So you shall;
And where th' offense is, let the great axe fall.
I pray you go with me.   *Exeunt.*

*

194 *poll* head 198 *of* on 204 *collateral* indirect 205 *touched* i.e. with the
crime 212 *trophy* memorial; *hatchment* coat of arms 213 *ostentation*
ceremony 215 *That* so that

Enter Horatio and others.   IV, vi

HORATIO What are they that would speak with me?

GENTLEMAN Seafaring men, sir. They say they have
    letters for you.

HORATIO Let them come in.   *[Exit Attendant.]*
    I do not know from what part of the world
    I should be greeted, if not from Lord Hamlet.
        Enter Sailors.

SAILOR God bless you, sir.

HORATIO Let him bless thee too.

SAILOR 'A shall, sir, an't please him. There's a letter for
    you, sir – it came from th' ambassador that was bound
    for England – if your name be Horatio, as I am let to
    know it is.

HORATIO *[reads the letter]* 'Horatio, when thou shalt have
    overlooked this, give these fellows some means to the 14
    king. They have letters for him. Ere we were two days
    old at sea, a pirate of very warlike appointment gave us 16
    chase. Finding ourselves too slow of sail, we put on a
    compelled valor, and in the grapple I boarded them. On
    the instant they got clear of our ship; so I alone became
    their prisoner. They have dealt with me like thieves of 20
    mercy, but they knew what they did: I am to do a good
    turn for them. Let the king have the letters I have sent,
    and repair thou to me with as much speed as thou
    wouldest fly death. I have words to speak in thine ear will
    make thee dumb; yet are they much too light for the bore 25
    of the matter. These good fellows will bring thee where I
    am. Rosencrantz and Guildenstern hold their course for
    England. Of them I have much to tell thee. Farewell.
                    'He that thou knowest thine, Hamlet.'

Come, I will give you way for these your letters,

IV, vi A chamber in the Castle   14 *overlooked* surveyed, scanned; *means*
i.e. of access   16 *appointment* equipment   20–21 *thieves of mercy* merciful
thieves   25 *bore* caliber (as of a gun)

And do't the speedier that you may direct me
To him from whom you brought them.   *Exeunt.*

*

IV, vii   *Enter King and Laertes.*

KING

Now must your conscience my acquittance seal,
And you must put me in your heart for friend,
Sith you have heard, and with a knowing ear,
That he which hath your noble father slain
Pursued my life.

LAERTES   It well appears. But tell me
6 Why you proceeded not against these feats
7 So crimeful and so capital in nature,
As by your safety, wisdom, all things else,
9 You mainly were stirred up.

KING   O, for two special reasons,
Which may to you perhaps seem much unsinewed,
But yet to me they're strong. The queen his mother
Lives almost by his looks, and for myself –
My virtue or my plague, be it either which –
14 She is so conjunctive to my life and soul
That, as the star moves not but in his sphere,
I could not but by her. The other motive
17 Why to a public count I might not go
18 Is the great love the general gender bear him,
Who, dipping all his faults in their affection,
Would, like the spring that turneth wood to stone,
21 Convert his gyves to graces ; so that my arrows,
Too slightly timbered for so loud a wind,
Would have reverted to my bow again,
And not where I had aimed them.

IV, vii A chamber in the Castle **6** *feats* deeds **7** *capital* punishable by
death **9** *mainly* powerfully **14** *conjunctive* closely united **17** *count* trial,
accounting **18** *general gender* common people **21** *gyves* fetters

LAERTES

And so have I a noble father lost,

A sister driven into desp'rate terms,   26

Whose worth, if praises may go back again,   27

Stood challenger on mount of all the age   28

For her perfections. But my revenge will come.

KING

Break not your sleeps for that. You must not think

That we are made of stuff so flat and dull

That we can let our beard be shook with danger,

And think it pastime. You shortly shall hear more.

I loved your father, and we love ourself,

And that, I hope, will teach you to imagine –

    Enter a Messenger with letters.

[How now? What news?]

MESSENGER   [Letters, my lord, from Hamlet:]

These to your majesty, this to the queen.

KING

From Hamlet? Who brought them?

MESSENGER

Sailors, my lord, they say; I saw them not.

They were given me by Claudio; he received them

Of him that brought them.

KING   Laertes, you shall hear them. –

Leave us.   *[Exit Messenger.]*

[Reads] 'High and mighty, you shall know I am set naked   43

on your kingdom. To-morrow shall I beg leave to see

your kingly eyes; when I shall (first asking your pardon

thereunto) recount the occasion of my sudden and more

strange return.   Hamlet.'

What should this mean? Are all the rest come back?

Or is it some abuse, and no such thing?   49

LAERTES

Know you the hand?

---

26 *terms* circumstances   **27** *back again* i.e. to her better circumstances   **28**
on mount on a height   **43** *naked* destitute   **49** *abuse* imposture

50 KING   'Tis Hamlet's character. 'Naked'!
    And in a postscript here, he says 'alone.'
52 Can you devise me?

LAERTES
    I am lost in it, my lord. But let him come.
    It warms the very sickness in my heart
    That I shall live and tell him to his teeth,
    'Thus diddest thou.'

KING   If it be so, Laertes,
    (As how should it be so? how otherwise?)
    Will you be ruled by me?

LAERTES   Ay, my lord,
    So you will not o'errule me to a peace.

KING
    To thine own peace. If he be now returned,
61 As checking at his voyage, and that he means
    No more to undertake it, I will work him
    To an exploit now ripe in my device,
    Under the which he shall not choose but fall;
    And for his death no wind of blame shall breathe,
66 But even his mother shall uncharge the practice
    And call it accident.

LAERTES   My lord, I will be ruled;
    The rather if you could devise it so
69 That I might be the organ.

KING   It falls right.
    You have been talked of since your travel much,
    And that in Hamlet's hearing, for a quality
    Wherein they say you shine. Your sum of parts
    Did not together pluck such envy from him
    As did that one, and that, in my regard,
75 Of the unworthiest siege.

LAERTES   What part is that, my lord?

50 *character* handwriting 52 *devise* explain to 61 *checking at* turning aside
from (like a falcon turning from its quarry for other prey) 66 *uncharge the
practice* acquit the stratagem of being a plot 69 *organ* instrument 75 *siege*
seat, rank

KING
    A very riband in the cap of youth,   76
    Yet needful too, for youth no less becomes
    The light and careless livery that it wears   78
    Than settled age his sables and his weeds,   79
    Importing health and graveness. Two months since   80
    Here was a gentleman of Normandy.
    I have seen myself, and served against, the French,
    And they can well on horseback, but this gallant   83
    Had witchcraft in't. He grew unto his seat,
    And to such wondrous doing brought his horse
    As had he been incorpsed and demi-natured   86
    With the brave beast. So far he topped my thought   87
    That I, in forgery of shapes and tricks,   88
    Come short of what he did.
LAERTES   A Norman was't?
KING A Norman.
LAERTES
    Upon my life, Lamord.
KING   The very same.
LAERTES
    I know him well. He is the brooch indeed   92
    And gem of all the nation.
KING
    He made confession of you,   94
    And gave you such a masterly report
    For art and exercise in your defense,
    And for your rapier most especial,
    That he cried out 'twould be a sight indeed
    If one could match you. The scrimers of their nation   99

76 *riband* decoration   78 *livery* distinctive attire   79 *sables* dignified robes
richly furred with sable; *weeds* distinctive garments   80 *health* welfare,
prosperity   83 *can well* can perform well   86 *incorpsed* made one body;
demi-natured made sharer of nature half and half (as man shares with horse
in the centaur)   87 *topped* excelled; *thought* imagination of possibilities
88 *forgery* invention   92 *brooch* ornament   94 *made confession* admitted the
rival accomplishments   99 *scrimers* fencers

He swore had neither motion, guard, nor eye,
If you opposed them. Sir, this report of his
Did Hamlet so envenom with his envy
That he could nothing do but wish and beg
Your sudden coming o'er to play with you.
Now, out of this –

LAERTES   What out of this, my lord?

KING
Laertes, was your father dear to you?
Or are you like the painting of a sorrow,
A face without a heart?

LAERTES   Why ask you this?

KING
Not that I think you did not love your father,
But that I know love is begun by time,
111   And that I see, in passages of proof,
112   Time qualifies the spark and fire of it.
There lives within the very flame of love
114   A kind of wick or snuff that will abate it,
115   And nothing is at a like goodness still,
116   For goodness, growing to a plurisy,
Dies in his own too-much. That we would do
We should do when we would, for this 'would' changes,
And hath abatements and delays as many
As there are tongues, are hands, are accidents,
And then this 'should' is like a spendthrift sigh,
122   That hurts by easing. But to the quick o' th' ulcer –
Hamlet comes back; what would you undertake
To show yourself your father's son in deed
More than in words?

LAERTES   To cut his throat i' th' church!

---

111 *passages of proof* incidents of experience   112 *qualifies* weakens   114
snuff unconsumed portion of the burned wick   115 *still* always   116 *plurisy*
excess   122 *hurts* i.e. shortens life by drawing blood from the heart (as was
believed); *quick* sensitive flesh

KING
    No place indeed should murder sanctuarize;   126
    Revenge should have no bounds. But, good Laertes,
    Will you do this? Keep close within your chamber.
    Hamlet returned shall know you are come home.
    We'll put on those shall praise your excellence   130
    And set a double varnish on the fame
    The Frenchman gave you, bring you in fine together   132
    And wager on your heads. He, being remiss,   133
    Most generous, and free from all contriving,
    Will not peruse the foils, so that with ease,   135
    Or with a little shuffling, you may choose
    A sword unbated, and, in a pass of practice,   137
    Requite him for your father.
LAERTES   I will do't,
    And for that purpose I'll anoint my sword.
    I bought an unction of a mountebank,   140
    So mortal that, but dip a knife in it,
    Where it draws blood no cataplasm so rare,   142
    Collected from all simples that have virtue   143
    Under the moon, can save the thing from death
    That is but scratched withal. I'll touch my point   145
    With this contagion, that, if I gall him slightly,   146
    It may be death.
KING   Let's further think of this,
    Weigh what convenience both of time and means
    May fit us to our shape. If this should fail,   149
    And that our drift look through our bad performance,   150
    'Twere better not assayed. Therefore this project
    Should have a back or second, that might hold

126 *sanctuarize* protect from punishment, give sanctuary to 130 *put on* instigate 132 *in fine* finally 133 *remiss* negligent 135 *peruse* scan 137 *unbated* not blunted; *pass of practice* thrust made effective by trickery 140 *unction* ointment; *mountebank* quack-doctor 142 *cataplasm* poultice 143 *simples* herbs 145 *withal* with it 146 *gall* scratch 149 *shape* plan 150 *drift* intention; *look* show

153   If this did blast in proof. Soft, let me see.
       We'll make a solemn wager on your cunnings –
       I ha't !
       When in your motion you are hot and dry –
       As make your bouts more violent to that end –
158   And that he calls for drink, I'll have preferred him
159   A chalice for the nonce, whereon but sipping,
160   If he by chance escape your venomed stuck,
       Our purpose may hold there. – But stay, what noise ?
            Enter Queen.

QUEEN
       One woe doth tread upon another's heel,
       So fast they follow. Your sister's drowned, Laertes.
LAERTES   Drowned ! O, where ?
QUEEN
165   There is a willow grows askant the brook,
166   That shows his hoar leaves in the glassy stream.
       Therewith fantastic garlands did she make
       Of crowflowers, nettles, daisies, and long purples,
169   That liberal shepherds give a grosser name,
       But our cold maids do dead men's fingers call them.
171   There on the pendent boughs her crownet weeds
       Clamb'ring to hang, an envious sliver broke,
       When down her weedy trophies and herself
       Fell in the weeping brook. Her clothes spread wide,
       And mermaid-like awhile they bore her up,
176   Which time she chanted snatches of old lauds,
177   As one incapable of her own distress,
178   Or like a creature native and indued
       Unto that element. But long it could not be
       Till that her garments, heavy with their drink,
       Pulled the poor wretch from her melodious lay
       To muddy death.

153 *blast in proof* burst during trial (like a faulty cannon)   158 *preferred*
offered   159 *nonce* occasion   160 *stuck* thrust   165 *askant* alongside   166
hoar grey   169 *liberal* free-spoken, licentious   171 *crownet* coronet   176
lauds hymns   177 *incapable of* insensible to   178 *indued* endowed

LAERTES   Alas, then she is drowned?

QUEEN Drowned, drowned.

LAERTES
Too much of water hast thou, poor Ophelia,
And therefore I forbid my tears; but yet
It is our trick; nature her custom holds,   186
Let shame say what it will. When these are gone,
The woman will be out. Adieu, my lord.   188
I have a speech o' fire, that fain would blaze
But that this folly drowns it.   *Exit.*

KING   Let's follow, Gertrude.
How much I had to do to calm his rage!
Now fear I this will give it start again;
Therefore let's follow.   *Exeunt.*

*

Enter two Clowns.   V, i

CLOWN Is she to be buried in Christian burial when she   1
willfully seeks her own salvation?

OTHER I tell thee she is. Therefore make her grave straight. 3
The crowner hath sate on her, and finds it Christian   4
burial.

CLOWN How can that be, unless she drowned herself in
her own defense?

OTHER Why, 'tis found so.

CLOWN It must be *se offendendo*; it cannot be else. For   8
here lies the point: if I drown myself wittingly, it argues
an act, and an act hath three branches – it is to act, to do,
and to perform. Argal, she drowned herself wittingly.   11

186 *trick* way (i.e. to shed tears when sorrowful)   188 *woman* unmanly part
of nature.
V, i A churchyard   s.d. *Clowns* rustics   1 *in Christian burial* in conse-
crated ground with the prescribed service of the Church (a burial denied to
suicides)   3 *straight* straightway, at once   4 *crowner* coroner   8 *se offendendo* a clownish transformation of '*se defendendo*,' 'in self-defense'   11
Argal for '*ergo*,' 'therefore'

12 OTHER Nay, but hear you, Goodman Delver.

CLOWN Give me leave. Here lies the water – good. Here
stands the man – good. If the man go to this water and
15　drown himself, it is, will he nill he, he goes, mark you
that. But if the water come to him and drown him, he
drowns not himself. Argal, he that is not guilty of his
own death shortens not his own life.

OTHER But is this law?

20 CLOWN Ay marry, is't – crowner's quest law.

OTHER Will you ha' the truth on't? If this had not been a
gentlewoman, she should have been buried out o'
Christian burial.

24 CLOWN Why, there thou say'st. And the more pity that
25　great folk should have count'nance in this world to
26　drown or hang themselves more than their even-
Christen. Come, my spade. There is no ancient gentlemen but gard'ners, ditchers, and grave-makers. They
hold up Adam's profession.

OTHER Was he a gentleman?

CLOWN 'A was the first that ever bore arms.

32 [OTHER Why, he had none.

CLOWN What, art a heathen? How dost thou understand
the Scripture? The Scripture says Adam digged. Could
he dig without arms?] I'll put another question to thee.
If thou answerest me not to the purpose, confess thyself –

OTHER Go to.

CLOWN What is he that builds stronger than either the
mason, the shipwright, or the carpenter?

OTHER The gallows-maker, for that frame outlives a
thousand tenants.

CLOWN I like thy wit well, in good faith. The gallows
does well. But how does it well? It does well to those
that do ill. Now thou dost ill to say the gallows is built

12 *Delver* Digger　15 *will he nill he* willy-nilly　20 *quest* inquest　24 *thou
say'st* you have it right　25 *count'nance* privilege　26 *even-Christen* fellow
Christian　32 *had none* i.e. had no gentleman's coat of arms

stronger than the church. Argal, the gallows may do
well to thee. To't again, come.

OTHER Who builds stronger than a mason, a shipwright,
or a carpenter?

CLOWN Ay, tell me that, and unyoke.   49

OTHER Marry, now I can tell.

CLOWN To't.

OTHER Mass, I cannot tell.   52

CLOWN Cudgel thy brains no more about it, for your dull
ass will not mend his pace with beating. And when you
are asked this question next, say 'a grave-maker.' The
houses he makes last till doomsday. Go, get thee in, and
fetch me a stoup of liquor.   *[Exit Other Clown.]* 57
Enter Hamlet and Horatio [as Clown digs and sings].

Song.

> In youth when I did love, did love,
>   Methought it was very sweet
> To contract – O – the time for – a – my behove,   60
>   O, methought there – a – was nothing – a – meet.

HAMLET Has this fellow no feeling of his business, that 'a
sings at grave-making?

HORATIO Custom hath made it in him a property of easi- 64
ness.

HAMLET 'Tis e'en so. The hand of little employment
hath the daintier sense.   66

CLOWN   *Song.*

> But age with his stealing steps
>   Hath clawed me in his clutch,
> And hath shipped me intil the land,
>   As if I had never been such.   69

[Throws up a skull.]

---

49 *unyoke* i.e. unharness your powers of thought after a good day's work
52 *Mass* by the Mass   **57** *stoup* large mug   **60** *behove* behoof, benefit   **64**
property peculiarity; *easiness* easy acceptability   **66** *daintier sense* more
delicate feeling (because the hand is less calloused)   **69** *intil* into

HAMLET That skull had a tongue in it, and could sing
72 once. How the knave jowls it to the ground, as if 'twere
Cain's jawbone, that did the first murder! This might be
74 the pate of a politician, which this ass now o'erreaches;
one that would circumvent God, might it not?

HORATIO It might, my lord.

HAMLET Or of a courtier, which could say 'Good morrow, sweet lord! How dost thou, sweet lord? This
might be my Lord Such-a-one, that praised my Lord
Such-a-one's horse when 'a meant to beg it, might it
not?

HORATIO Ay, my lord.

82 HAMLET Why, e'en so, and now my Lady Worm's, chap-
83 less, and knocked about the mazzard with a sexton's
spade. Here's fine revolution, an we had the trick to
see't. Did these bones cost no more the breeding but to
86 play at loggets with 'em? Mine ache to think on't.

CLOWN   *Song.*

A pickaxe and a spade, a spade,
88   For and a shrouding sheet;
O, a pit of clay for to be made
For such a guest is meet.

[Throws up another skull.]

HAMLET There's another. Why may not that be the skull
92 of a lawyer? Where be his quiddities now, his quillities,
93 his cases, his tenures, and his tricks? Why does he suffer
94 this mad knave now to knock him about the sconce with
a dirty shovel, and will not tell him of his action of
battery? Hum! This fellow might be in's time a great
97 buyer of land, with his statutes, his recognizances, his

72 *jowls* hurls   74 *politician* crafty schemer; *o'erreaches* gets the better of
(with a play upon the literal meaning)   82 *chapless* lacking the lower chap or
jaw   83 *mazzard* head   86 *loggets* small pieces of wood thrown in a game
88 *For and* and   92 *quiddities* subtleties (from scholastic '*quidditas*,' meaning the distinctive nature of anything); *quillities* nice distinctions   93
tenures holdings of property   94 *sconce* head   97 *statutes, recognizances* legal
documents or bonds acknowledging debt

fines, his double vouchers, his recoveries. [Is this the fine 98
of his fines, and the recovery of his recoveries,] to have
his fine pate full of fine dirt? Will his vouchers vouch him
no more of his purchases, and double ones too, than the
length and breadth of a pair of indentures? The very con- 102
veyances of his lands will scarcely lie in this box, and
must th' inheritor himself have no more, ha?

HORATIO Not a jot more, my lord.

HAMLET Is not parchment made of sheepskins?

HORATIO Ay, my lord, and of calveskins too.

HAMLET They are sheep and calves which seek out assurance in that. I will speak to this fellow. Whose grave's
this, sirrah?

CLOWN Mine, sir.

[Sings]   O, a pit of clay for to be made
                For such a guest is meet.

HAMLET I think it be thine indeed, for thou liest in't.

CLOWN You lie out on't, sir, and therefore 'tis not yours.
For my part, I do not lie in't, yet it is mine.

HAMLET Thou dost lie in't, to be in't and say it is thine.
'Tis for the dead, not for the quick; therefore thou liest. 118

CLOWN 'Tis a quick lie, sir; 'twill away again from me to
you.

HAMLET What man dost thou dig it for?

CLOWN For no man, sir.

HAMLET What woman then?

CLOWN For none neither.

HAMLET Who is to be buried in't?

CLOWN One that was a woman, sir; but, rest her soul,
she's dead.

HAMLET How absolute the knave is! We must speak by 128

---

98 *fines, recoveries* modes of converting estate tail into fee simple; *vouchers*
persons vouched or called on to warrant a title; *fine* end (introducing a
word play involving four meanings of 'fine')   102 *pair of indentures* deed
or legal agreement in duplicate; *conveyances* deeds   118 *quick* living   128
absolute positive   128-29 *by the card* by the card on which the points of
the mariner's compass are marked, absolutely to the point

129 the card, or equivocation will undo us. By the Lord,
Horatio, this three years I have taken note of it, the age
131 is grown so picked that the toe of the peasant comes so
132 near the heel of the courtier he galls his kibe. – How long
hast thou been a grave-maker?

CLOWN Of all the days i' th' year, I came to't that day that
our last king Hamlet overcame Fortinbras.

HAMLET How long is that since?

CLOWN Cannot you tell that? Every fool can tell that. It
was the very day that young Hamlet was born – he that
is mad, and sent into England.

140 HAMLET Ay, marry, why was he sent into England?

CLOWN Why, because 'a was mad. 'A shall recover his
wits there; or, if 'a do not, 'tis no great matter there.

HAMLET Why?

CLOWN 'Twill not be seen in him there. There the men
are as mad as he.

HAMLET How came he mad?

CLOWN Very strangely, they say.

HAMLET How strangely?

CLOWN Faith, e'en with losing his wits.

HAMLET Upon what ground?

CLOWN Why, here in Denmark. I have been sexton here,
man and boy, thirty years.

HAMLET How long will a man lie i' th' earth ere he rot?

CLOWN Faith, if 'a be not rotten before 'a die (as we have
155 many pocky corses now-a-days that will scarce hold the
laying in), 'a will last you some eight year or nine year.
A tanner will last you nine year.

HAMLET Why he more than another?

CLOWN Why, sir, his hide is so tanned with his trade that
'a will keep out water a great while, and your water is a
sore decayer of your whoreson dead body. Here's a skull
now hath lien you i' th' earth three-and-twenty years.

129 *equivocation* ambiguity 131 *picked* refined, spruce 132 *galls* chafes;
kibe chilblain 155 *pocky* rotten (literally, corrupted by pox, or syphilis)

HAMLET Whose was it?

CLOWN A whoreson mad fellow's it was. Whose do you
think it was?

HAMLET Nay, I know not.

CLOWN A pestilence on him for a mad rogue! 'A poured a
flagon of Rhenish on my head once. This same skull, sir,   168
was – sir – Yorick's skull, the king's jester.

HAMLET This?

CLOWN E'en that.

HAMLET Let me see. [Takes the skull.] Alas, poor Yorick!
I knew him, Horatio, a fellow of infinite jest, of most excellent fancy. He hath borne me on his back a thousand
times. And now how abhorred in my imagination it is!
My gorge rises at it. Here hung those lips that I have
kissed I know not how oft. Where be your gibes now?
Your gambols, your songs, your flashes of merriment
that were wont to set the table on a roar? Not one now to
mock your own grinning? Quite chapfall'n? Now get   180
you to my lady's chamber, and tell her, let her paint an
inch thick, to this favor she must come. Make her laugh   182
at that. Prithee, Horatio, tell me one thing.

HORATIO What's that, my lord?

HAMLET Dost thou think Alexander looked o' this fashion
i' th' earth?

HORATIO E'en so.

HAMLET And smelt so? Pah!
[Puts down the skull.]

HORATIO E'en so, my lord.

HAMLET To what base uses we may return, Horatio!
Why may not imagination trace the noble dust of
Alexander till 'a find it stopping a bunghole?

HORATIO 'Twere to consider too curiously, to consider so.   193

HAMLET No, faith, not a jot, but to follow him thither with
modesty enough, and likelihood to lead it; as thus: 195

168 *Rhenish* Rhine wine   180 *chapfall'n* lacking the lower shap, or jaw (with
a play on the sense 'down in the mouth,' 'dejected')   182 *favor* countenance,
aspect   193 *curiously* minutely   195 *modesty* moderation

Alexander died, Alexander was buried, Alexander re-
turneth to dust; the dust is earth; of earth we make loam;
and why of that loam whereto he was converted might
they not stop a beer barrel?

200   Imperious Caesar, dead and turned to clay,
       Might stop a hole to keep the wind away.
       O, that that earth which kept the world in awe
203   Should patch a wall t' expel the winter's flaw!
       But soft, but soft awhile! Here comes the king –
                Enter King, Queen, Laertes, and the Corse [with
                Lords attendant and a Doctor of Divinity as Priest].
       The queen, the courtiers. Who is this they follow?
       And with such maimèd rites? This doth betoken
       The corse they follow did with desp'rate hand
208   Fordo it own life. 'Twas of some estate.
209   Couch we awhile, and mark.
                [Retires with Horatio.]

LAERTES
       What ceremony else?
HAMLET   That is Laertes,
       A very noble youth. Mark.
LAERTES
       What ceremony else?
DOCTOR
       Her obsequies have been as far enlarged
       As we have warranty. Her death was doubtful,
       And, but that great command o'ersways the order,
       She should in ground unsanctified have lodged
       Till the last trumpet. For charitable prayers,
218   Shards, flints, and pebbles should be thrown on her.
219   Yet here she is allowed her virgin crants,
220   Her maiden strewments, and the bringing home
       Of bell and burial.

200 *Imperious* imperial   203 *flaw* gust of wind   208 *Fordo* destroy; *it* its;
estate rank   209 *Couch* hide   218 *Shards* broken pieces of pottery   219
crants garland   220 *strewments* strewings of the grave with flowers;
bringing home laying to rest

LAERTES
  Must there no more be done ?
DOCTOR   No more be done.
  We should profane the service of the dead
  To sing a requiem and such rest to her
  As to peace-parted souls.
LAERTES   Lay her i' th' earth,
  And from her fair and unpolluted flesh
  May violets spring ! I tell thee, churlish priest,
  A minist'ring angel shall my sister be
  When thou liest howling.
HAMLET   What, the fair Ophelia ?
QUEEN
  Sweets to the sweet ! Farewell.
    [Scatters flowers.]
  I hoped thou shouldst have been my Hamlet's wife.
  I thought thy bride-bed to have decked, sweet maid,
  And not have strewed thy grave.
LAERTES   O, treble woe
  Fall ten times treble on that cursèd head
  Whose wicked deed thy most ingenious sense   235
  Deprived thee of ! Hold off the earth awhile,
  Till I have caught her once more in mine arms.
    [Leaps in the grave.]
  Now pile your dust upon the quick and dead
  Till of this flat a mountain you have made
  T' o'ertop old Pelion or the skyish head   240
  Of blue Olympus.
HAMLET *[coming forward]*   What is he whose grief
  Bears such an emphasis ? whose phrase of sorrow
  Conjures the wand'ring stars, and makes them stand   243

---

235 *most ingenious* of quickest apprehension   **240** *Pelion* a mountain in
Thessaly, like Olympus and also Ossa (the allusion being to the war in
which the Titans fought the gods and attempted to heap Ossa and Olympus
on Pelion, or Pelion and Ossa on Olympus, in order to scale heaven)   **243**
Conjures charms, puts a spell upon; *wand'ring stars* planets

Like wonder-wounded hearers? This is I,
Hamlet the Dane.
    [Leaps in after Laertes.]

LAERTES   The devil take thy soul!
    [Grapples with him.]

HAMLET
Thou pray'st not well.
I prithee take thy fingers from my throat,
248   For, though I am not splenitive and rash,
Yet have I in me something dangerous,
Which let thy wisdom fear. Hold off thy hand.

KING
Pluck them asunder.

QUEEN   Hamlet, Hamlet!

ALL
Gentlemen!

HORATIO   Good my lord, be quiet.
    *[Attendants part them, and they come out of the
    grave.]*

HAMLET
Why, I will fight with him upon this theme
Until my eyelids will no longer wag.

QUEEN
O my son, what theme?

HAMLET
I loved Ophelia. Forty thousand brothers
Could not with all their quantity of love
Make up my sum. What wilt thou do for her?

KING
O, he is mad, Laertes.

QUEEN
For love of God, forbear him.

HAMLET
'Swounds, show me what thou't do.

---

248 *splenitive* of fiery temper (the spleen being considered the seat of anger)

Woo't weep? woo't fight? woo't fast? woo't tear thyself? 262
Woo't drink up esill? eat a crocodile? 263
I'll do't. Dost thou come here to whine?
To outface me with leaping in her grave?
Be buried quick with her, and so will I. 266
And if thou prate of mountains, let them throw
Millions of acres on us, till our ground,
Singeing his pate against the burning zone,
Make Ossa like a wart! Nay, an thou'lt mouth,
I'll rant as well as thou.

QUEEN   This is mere madness; 271
And thus a while the fit will work on him.
Anon, as patient as the female dove
When that her golden couplets are disclosed, 274
His silence will sit drooping.

HAMLET   Hear you, sir.
What is the reason that you use me thus?
I loved you ever. But it is no matter.
Let Hercules himself do what he may,
The cat will mew, and dog will have his day.

KING
I pray thee, good Horatio, wait upon him.
                              Exit Hamlet and Horatio.
    [*To Laertes*]
Strengthen your patience in our last night's speech. 281
We'll put the matter to the present push. – 282
Good Gertrude, set some watch over your son. –
This grave shall have a living monument.
An hour of quiet shortly shall we see;
Till then in patience our proceeding be.   *Exeunt.*

*

262 *Woo't* wilt (thou) 263 *esill* vinegar 266 *quick* alive 271 *mere*
absolute 274 *couplets* pair of fledglings; *disclosed* hatched 281 *in* by call-
ing to mind 282 *present push* immediate trial

V, ii   *Enter Hamlet and Horatio.*

HAMLET

So much for this, sir; now shall you see the other.
You do remember all the circumstance?

HORATIO

Remember it, my lord!

HAMLET

Sir, in my heart there was a kind of fighting
That would not let me sleep. Methought I lay

6 Worse than the mutines in the bilboes. Rashly,
And praised be rashness for it – let us know,
Our indiscretion sometime serves us well

9 When our deep plots do pall, and that should learn us
There's a divinity that shapes our ends,

11 Rough-hew them how we will –

HORATIO   That is most certain.

HAMLET

Up from my cabin,
My sea-gown scarfed about me, in the dark
Groped I to find out them, had my desire,

15 Fingered their packet, and in fine withdrew
To mine own room again, making so bold,
My fears forgetting manners, to unseal
Their grand commission; where I found, Horatio –
Ah, royal knavery! – an exact command,

20 Larded with many several sorts of reasons,

21 Importing Denmark's health, and England's too,

22 With, ho! such bugs and goblins in my life,

23 That on the supervise, no leisure bated,
No, not to stay the grinding of the axe,
My head should be struck off.

HORATIO   Is't possible?

V, ii The hall of the Castle   6 *mutines* mutineers; *bilboes* fetters   9 *pall* fail   11 *Rough-hew* shape roughly in trial form   15 *Fingered* filched; *in fine* finally   20 *Larded* enriched   21 *Importing* relating to   22 *bugs* bugbears; *in my life* to be encountered as dangers if I should be allowed to live   23 *supervise* perusal; *bated* deducted, allowed

HAMLET
　Here's the commission; read it at more leisure.
　But wilt thou hear me how I did proceed?

HORATIO　I beseech you.

HAMLET
　Being thus benetted round with villainies,
　Or I could make a prologue to my brains,   30
　They had begun the play. I sat me down,
　Devised a new commission, wrote it fair.
　I once did hold it, as our statists do,   33
　A baseness to write fair, and labored much   34
　How to forget that learning, but, sir, now
　It did me yeoman's service. Wilt thou know   36
　Th' effect of what I wrote?   37

HORATIO　　　　　　　　Ay, good my lord.

HAMLET
　An earnest conjuration from the king,
　As England was his faithful tributary,
　As love between them like the palm might flourish,
　As peace should still her wheaten garland wear   41
　And stand a comma 'tween their amities,   42
　And many such-like as's of great charge,   43
　That on the view and knowing of these contents,
　Without debatement further, more or less,
　He should the bearers put to sudden death,
　Not shriving time allowed.   47

HORATIO　　　　　　　　How was this sealed?

HAMLET
　Why, even in that was heaven ordinant.   48
　I had my father's signet in my purse,

---

30 *Or* ere　33 *statists* statesmen　34 *fair* with professional clarity (like a
clerk or a scrivener, not like a gentleman)　36 *yeoman's service* stout service
such as yeomen footsoldiers gave as archers　37 *effect* purport　41 *wheaten
garland* adornment of fruitful agriculture　42 *comma* connective (because
it indicates continuity of thought in a sentence)　43 *charge* burden (with a
double meaning to fit a play that makes *as's* into 'asses')　47 *shriving time*
time for confession and absolution　48 *ordinant* controlling

50   Which was the model of that Danish seal,
      Folded the writ up in the form of th' other,
52   Subscribed it, gave't th' impression, placed it safely,
      The changeling never known. Now, the next day
54   Was our sea-fight, and what to this was sequent
      Thou know'st already.

HORATIO
      So Guildenstern and Rosencrantz go to't.

HAMLET
      [Why, man, they did make love to this employment.]
      They are not near my conscience; their defeat
59   Does by their own insinuation grow.
      'Tis dangerous when the baser nature comes
61   Between the pass and fell incensèd points
      Of mighty opposites.

HORATIO   Why, what a king is this!

HAMLET
63   Does it not, think thee, stand me now upon –
      He that hath killed my king, and whored my mother,
65   Popped in between th' election and my hopes,
66   Thrown out his angle for my proper life,
67   And with such coz'nage – is't not perfect conscience
68   [To quit him with this arm? And is't not to be damned
69   To let this canker of our nature come
      In further evil?

HORATIO
      It must be shortly known to him from England
      What is the issue of the business there.

HAMLET
      It will be short; the interim is mine,
      And a man's life 's no more than to say 'one.'
      But I am very sorry, good Horatio,

50 *model* counterpart   52 *impression* i.e. of the signet   54 *sequent* subsequent   59 *insinuation* intrusion   61 *pass* thrust; *fell* fierce   63 *stand* rest incumbent   65 *election* i.e. to the kingship (the Danish kingship being elective)   66 *angle* fishing line; *proper* own   67 *coz'nage* cozenage, trickery   68 *quit* repay   69 *canker* cancer, ulcer

That to Laertes I forgot myself,
For by the image of my cause I see
The portraiture of his. I'll court his favors.
But sure the bravery of his grief did put me   79
Into a tow'ring passion.

HORATIO   Peace, who comes here?]

Enter [Osric,] a courtier.

OSRIC Your lordship is right welcome back to Denmark.

HAMLET I humbly thank you, sir. *[aside to Horatio]* Dost know this waterfly?

HORATIO *[aside to Hamlet]* No, my good lord.

HAMLET *[aside to Horatio]* Thy state is the more gracious, for 'tis a vice to know him. He hath much land, and fertile. Let a beast be lord of beasts, and his crib shall stand at the king's mess. 'Tis a chough, but, as I say, 88 spacious in the possession of dirt.

OSRIC Sweet lord, if your lordship were at leisure, I should impart a thing to you from his majesty.

HAMLET I will receive it, sir, with all diligence of spirit. Put your bonnet to his right use. 'Tis for the head.

OSRIC I thank your lordship, it is very hot.

HAMLET No, believe me, 'tis very cold; the wind is northerly.

OSRIC It is indifferent cold, my lord, indeed.   97

HAMLET But yet methinks it is very sultry and hot for my complexion.   99

OSRIC Exceedingly, my lord; it is very sultry, as 'twere –
I cannot tell how. But, my lord, his majesty bade me signify to you that 'a has laid a great wager on your head. Sir, this is the matter –

HAMLET I beseech you remember.   104

[Hamlet moves him to put on his hat.]

---

79 *bravery* ostentatious display   88 *mess* table; *chough* jackdaw, chatterer
97 *indifferent* somewhat   99 *complexion* temperament   104 *remember* i.e.
remember you have done all that courtesy demands

105 OSRIC Nay, good my lord; for mine ease, in good faith.
      Sir, here is newly come to court Laertes – believe me, an
107 absolute gentleman, full of most excellent differences, of
108 very soft society and great showing. Indeed, to speak
109 feelingly of him, he is the card or calendar of gentry; for
110 you shall find in him the continent of what part a
      gentleman would see.
112 HAMLET Sir, his definement suffers no perdition in you,
113 though, I know, to divide him inventorially would dozy
114 th' arithmetic of memory, and yet but yaw neither in re-
      spect of his quick sail. But, in the verity of extolment, I
116 take him to be a soul of great article, and his infusion of
117 such dearth and rareness as, to make true diction of him,
118 his semblable is his mirror, and who else would trace
119 him, his umbrage, nothing more.
      OSRIC Your lordship speaks most infallibly of him.
121 HAMLET The concernancy, sir? Why do we wrap the
122 gentleman in our more rawer breath?
      OSRIC Sir?
      HORATIO Is't not possible to understand in another
125 tongue? You will to't, sir, really.
126 HAMLET What imports the nomination of this gentle-
      man?
      OSRIC Of Laertes?
      HORATIO [aside to Hamlet] His purse is empty already.
      All's golden words are spent.

105 *for mine ease* i.e. I keep my hat off just for comfort (a conventional polite
phrase)   107 *differences* differentiating characteristics, special qualities
108 *soft society* gentle manners; *great showing* noble appearance   109
feelingly appropriately; *card* map; *calendar* guide; *gentry* gentlemanliness
110 *continent* all-containing embodiment (with an implication of geo-
graphical continent to go with *card*)   112 *definement* definition; *perdition*
loss   113 *dozy* dizzy, stagger   114 *yaw* hold to a course unsteadily like a
ship that steers wild; *neither* for all that   114–15 *in respect of* in comparison
with   116 *article* scope, importance; *infusion* essence   117 *dearth* scarcity
118 *semblable* likeness (i.e. only true likeness); *trace* follow   119 *umbrage*
shadow   121 *concernancy* relevance   122 *rawer breath* cruder speech   125
to't i.e. get to an understanding   126 *nomination* mention

HAMLET Of him, sir.

OSRIC I know you are not ignorant –

HAMLET I would you did, sir; yet, in faith, if you did, it
would not much approve me. Well, sir?   133

OSRIC You are not ignorant of what excellence Laertes is –

HAMLET I dare not confess that, lest I should compare   135
with him in excellence; but to know a man well were to
know himself.

OSRIC I mean, sir, for his weapon; but in the imputation
laid on him by them, in his meed he's unfellowed.   139

HAMLET What's his weapon?

OSRIC Rapier and dagger.

HAMLET That's two of his weapons – but well.

OSRIC The king, sir, hath wagered with him six Barbary
horses, against the which he has impawned, as I take it,   144
six French rapiers and poniards, with their assigns, as   145
girdle, hangers, and so. Three of the carriages, in faith, 146
are very dear to fancy, very responsive to the hilts, most 147
delicate carriages, and of very liberal conceit.   148

HAMLET What call you the carriages?

HORATIO [aside to Hamlet] I knew you must be edified by
the margent ere you had done.   151

OSRIC The carriages, sir, are the hangers.

HAMLET The phrase would be more germane to the matter if we could carry a cannon by our sides. I would it
might be hangers till then. But on! Six Barbary horses
against six French swords, their assigns, and three
liberal-conceited carriages – that's the French bet
against the Danish. Why is this all impawned, as you
call it?

OSRIC The king, sir, hath laid, sir, that in a dozen passes

---

133 *approve me* be to my credit   **135** *compare* compete   **139** *meed* worth
144 *impawned* staked   **145** *assigns* appurtenances   **146** *hangers* straps by
which the sword hangs from the belt   **147** *dear to fancy* finely designed;
responsive corresponding closely   **148** *liberal conceit* tasteful design, refined
conception   **151** *margent* margin (i.e. explanatory notes there printed)

between yourself and him he shall not exceed you three hits; he hath laid on twelve for nine, and it would come to immediate trial if your lordship would vouchsafe the answer.

HAMLET How if I answer no?

OSRIC I mean, my lord, the opposition of your person in trial.

HAMLET Sir, I will walk here in the hall. If it please his
168 majesty, it is the breathing time of day with me. Let the foils be brought, the gentleman willing, and the king
170 hold his purpose, I will win for him an I can; if not, I will gain nothing but my shame and the odd hits.

OSRIC Shall I redeliver you e'en so?

HAMLET To this effect, sir, after what flourish your nature will.

OSRIC I commend my duty to your lordship.

HAMLET Yours, yours. *[Exit Osric.]* He does well to commend it himself; there are no tongues else for's turn.

178 HORATIO This lapwing runs away with the shell on his head.

179 HAMLET 'A did comply, sir, with his dug before 'a sucked
180 it. Thus has he, and many more of the same bevy that I
181 know the drossy age dotes on, only got the tune of the time and, out of an habit of encounter, a kind of yeasty collection, which carries them through and through the
184 most fanned and winnowed opinions; and do but blow them to their trial, the bubbles are out.

        Enter a Lord.

LORD My lord, his majesty commended him to you by young Osric, who brings back to him that you attend him in the hall. He sends to know if your pleasure hold to play with Laertes, or that you will take longer time.

HAMLET I am constant to my purposes; they follow the

168 *breathing time* exercise hour   170 *an* if   178 *lapwing* a bird reputed to be so precocious as to run as soon as hatched   179 *comply* observe formalities of courtesy; *dug* mother's nipple   180 *bevy* company   181 *drossy* frivolous   184 *fanned and winnowed* select and refined

king's pleasure. If his fitness speaks, mine is ready; now
or whensoever, provided I be so able as now.

LORD The king and queen and all are coming down.

HAMLET In happy time.   194

LORD The queen desires you to use some gentle enter- 195
tainment to Laertes before you fall to play.

HAMLET She well instructs me.   [*Exit Lord.*]

HORATIO You will lose this wager, my lord.

HAMLET I do not think so. Since he went into France I
have been in continual practice. I shall win at the odds.
But thou wouldst not think how ill all's here about my
heart. But it is no matter.

HORATIO Nay, good my lord –

HAMLET It is but foolery, but it is such a kind of gain- 204
giving as would perhaps trouble a woman.

HORATIO If your mind dislike anything, obey it. I will
forestall their repair hither and say you are not fit.

HAMLET Not a whit, we defy augury. There is special
providence in the fall of a sparrow. If it be now, 'tis not
to come; if it be not to come, it will be now; if it be not
now, yet it will come. The readiness is all. Since no man 211
of aught he leaves knows, what is't to leave betimes? Let
be.

> *A table prepared. [Enter] Trumpets, Drums, and*
> *Officers with cushions; King, Queen, [Osric,] and all*
> *the State, [with] foils, daggers, [and stoups of wine*
> *borne in;] and Laertes.*

KING
Come, Hamlet, come, and take this hand from me.
    [*The King puts Laertes' hand into Hamlet's.*]

HAMLET
Give me your pardon, sir. I have done you wrong,
But pardon't, as you are a gentleman.
This presence knows, and you must needs have heard, 217

---

194 *In happy time* I am happy (a polite response)   195 *entertainment* words
of reception or greeting   204 *gaingiving* misgiving   211 *all* all that
matters   217 *presence* assembly

How I am punished with a sore distraction.
What I have done
220   That might your nature, honor, and exception
Roughly awake, I here proclaim was madness.
Was't Hamlet wronged Laertes? Never Hamlet.
If Hamlet from himself be ta'en away,
And when he's not himself does wrong Laertes,
Then Hamlet does it not, Hamlet denies it.
Who does it then? His madness. If't be so,
227   Hamlet is of the faction that is wronged;
His madness is poor Hamlet's enemy.
Sir, in this audience,
Let my disclaiming from a purposed evil
Free me so far in your most generous thoughts
That I have shot my arrow o'er the house
And hurt my brother.

233 LAERTES   I am satisfied in nature,
Whose motive in this case should stir me most
235   To my revenge. But in my terms of honor
I stand aloof, and will no reconcilement
Till by some elder masters of known honor
238   I have a voice and precedent of peace
239   To keep my name ungored. But till that time
I do receive your offered love like love,
And will not wrong it.

HAMLET   I embrace it freely,
And will this brother's wager frankly play.
Give us the foils. Come on.

LAERTES   Come, one for me.

HAMLET
244   I'll be your foil, Laertes. In mine ignorance
Your skill shall, like a star i' th' darkest night,

---

220 *exception* disapproval **227** *faction* body of persons taking a side in a
contention **233** *nature* natural feeling as a person **235** *terms of honor*
position as a man of honor **238** *voice* authoritative statement **239** *ungored*
uninjured **244** *foil* setting that displays a jewel advantageously (with a
play upon the meaning 'weapon')

Stick fiery off indeed.   246

LAERTES   You mock me, sir.

HAMLET

No, by this hand.

KING

Give them the foils, young Osric. Cousin Hamlet,
You know the wager?

HAMLET   Very well, my lord.
Your grace has laid the odds o' th' weaker side.

KING

I do not fear it, I have seen you both;
But since he is bettered, we have therefore odds.

LAERTES

This is too heavy; let me see another.

HAMLET

This likes me well. These foils have all a length?
    [Prepare to play.]

OSRIC

Ay, my good lord.

KING

Set me the stoups of wine upon that table.
If Hamlet give the first or second hit,
Or quit in answer of the third exchange,   258
Let all the battlements their ordnance fire.
The king shall drink to Hamlet's better breath,
And in the cup an union shall he throw   261
Richer than that which four successive kings
In Denmark's crown have worn. Give me the cups,
And let the kettle to the trumpet speak,   264
The trumpet to the cannoneer without,
The cannons to the heavens, the heaven to earth,
'Now the king drinks to Hamlet.' Come, begin.
        Trumpets the while.
And you, the judges, bear a wary eye.

246 *Stick fiery off* show in brilliant relief   258 *quit* repay by a hit   261 *union*
pearl   264 *kettle* kettledrum

HAMLET
  Come on, sir.
LAERTES   Come, my lord.
      [They play.]
HAMLET   One.
LAERTES   No.
HAMLET   Judgment?
OSRIC
  A hit, a very palpable hit.
          Drum, trumpets, and shot. Flourish; a piece goes off.
LAERTES   Well, again.
KING
  Stay, give me drink. Hamlet, this pearl is thine.
  Here's to thy health. Give him the cup.
HAMLET
  I'll play this bout first; set it by awhile.
  Come. *[They play.]* Another hit. What say you?
LAERTES
  A touch, a touch; I do confess't.
KING
  Our son shall win.
276 QUEEN   He's fat, and scant of breath.
277   Here, Hamlet, take my napkin, rub thy brows.
278   The queen carouses to thy fortune, Hamlet.
HAMLET
  Good madam!
KING   Gertrude, do not drink.
QUEEN
  I will, my lord; I pray you pardon me.
      [Drinks.]
KING *[aside]*
  It is the poisoned cup; it is too late.
HAMLET
  I dare not drink yet, madam – by and by.

276 *fat* not physically fit, out of training   277 *napkin* handkerchief   278
carouses drinks a toast

QUEEN
  Come, let me wipe thy face.

LAERTES
  My lord, I'll hit him now.

KING   I do not think't.

LAERTES [aside]
  And yet it is almost against my conscience.

HAMLET
  Come for the third, Laertes. You but dally.
  I pray you pass with your best violence;
  I am afeard you make a wanton of me.   288

LAERTES
  Say you so? Come on.
          [They play.]

OSRIC
  Nothing neither way.

LAERTES
  Have at you now!
          [In scuffling they change rapiers, and both are
          wounded with the poisoned weapon.]

KING   Part them. They are incensed.

HAMLET
  Nay, come – again!
          [The Queen falls.]

OSRIC   Look to the queen there, ho!

HORATIO
  They bleed on both sides. How is it, my lord?

OSRIC
  How is't, Laertes?

LAERTES
  Why, as a woodcock to mine own springe, Osric.   295
  I am justly killed with mine own treachery.

HAMLET
  How does the queen?

288 *wanton* pampered child   295 *woodcock* a bird reputed to be stupid and
easily trapped; *springe* trap

297 KING   She sounds to see them bleed.

QUEEN

No, no, the drink, the drink! O my dear Hamlet!
The drink, the drink! I am poisoned.
          [Dies.]

HAMLET

O villainy! Ho! let the door be locked.
Treachery! Seek it out.
          [Laertes falls.]

LAERTES

It is here, Hamlet. Hamlet, thou art slain;
No med'cine in the world can do thee good.
In thee there is not half an hour's life.
The treacherous instrument is in thy hand,
306   Unbated and envenomed. The foul practice
Hath turned itself on me. Lo, here I lie,
Never to rise again. Thy mother's poisoned.
I can no more. The king, the king's to blame.

HAMLET

The point envenomed too?
Then venom, to thy work.
          [Hurts the King.]

ALL Treason! treason!

KING

O, yet defend me, friends. I am but hurt.

HAMLET

Here, thou incestuous, murd'rous, damnèd Dane,
Drink off this potion. Is thy union here?
Follow my mother.
          [King dies.]

LAERTES   He is justly served.
317   It is a poison tempered by himself.
Exchange forgiveness with me, noble Hamlet.
Mine and my father's death come not upon thee,

---

297 *sounds* swoons **306** *Unbated* unblunted; *practice* stratagem **317**
tempered mixed

Nor thine on me!
   [Dies.]

HAMLET
Heaven make thee free of it! I follow thee.
I am dead, Horatio. Wretched queen, adieu!
You that look pale and tremble at this chance,
That are but mutes or audience to this act,   324
Had I but time – as this fell sergeant, Death,   325
Is strict in his arrest – O, I could tell you –
But let it be. Horatio, I am dead;
Thou livest; report me and my cause aright
To the unsatisfied.

HORATIO   Never believe it.
I am more an antique Roman than a Dane.
Here's yet some liquor left.

HAMLET   As th' art a man,
Give me the cup. Let go. By heaven, I'll ha't!
O God, Horatio, what a wounded name,
Things standing thus unknown, shall live behind me!
If thou didst ever hold me in thy heart,
Absent thee from felicity awhile,
And in this harsh world draw thy breath in pain,
To tell my story.
    A march afar off.
                 What warlike noise is this?

OSRIC
Young Fortinbras, with conquest come from Poland,
To the ambassadors of England gives
This warlike volley.

HAMLET   O, I die, Horatio!
The potent poison quite o'ercrows my spirit.   342
I cannot live to hear the news from England,
But I do prophesy th' election lights   344
On Fortinbras. He has my dying voice.   345

324 *mutes* actors in a play who speak no lines   325 *sergeant* sheriff's officer
342 *o'ercrows* triumphs over (like a victor in a cockfight)   344 *election* i.e. to
the throne   345 *voice* vote

346   So tell him, with th' occurrents, more and less,
347   Which have solicited – the rest is silence.
           Dies.

HORATIO
     Now cracks a noble heart. Good night, sweet prince,
     And flights of angels sing thee to thy rest!
           [*March within.*]
     Why does the drum come hither?
           *Enter Fortinbras, with the Ambassadors [and with
           his train of Drum, Colors, and Attendants].*

FORTINBRAS
     Where is this sight?

HORATIO   What is it you would see?
     If aught of woe or wonder, cease your search.

FORTINBRAS
353   This quarry cries on havoc. O proud Death,
354   What feast is toward in thine eternal cell
       That thou so many princes at a shot
       So bloodily hast struck?

AMBASSADOR   The sight is dismal;
     And our affairs from England come too late.
     The ears are senseless that should give us hearing
     To tell him his commandment is fulfilled,
     That Rosencrantz and Guildenstern are dead.
     Where should we have our thanks?

HORATIO   Not from his mouth,
     Had it th' ability of life to thank you.
     He never gave commandment for their death.
364   But since, so jump upon this bloody question,
       You from the Polack wars, and you from England,
       Are here arrived, give order that these bodies
367   High on a stage be placèd to the view,

---

346 *occurrents* occurrences   347 *solicited* incited, provoked   353 *quarry*
pile of dead (literally, of dead deer gathered after the hunt); *cries on* proclaims loudly; *havoc* indiscriminate killing and destruction such as would
follow the order 'havoc,' or 'pillage,' given to an army   354 *toward* forth-
coming   364 *jump* precisely   367 *stage* platform

And let me speak to th' yet unknowing world
How these things came about. So shall you hear
Of carnal, bloody, and unnatural acts,
Of accidental judgments, casual slaughters,   371
Of deaths put on by cunning and forced cause,   372
And, in this upshot, purposes mistook
Fall'n on th' inventors' heads. All this can I
Truly deliver.

FORTINBRAS   Let us haste to hear it,
And call the noblest to the audience.
For me, with sorrow I embrace my fortune.
I have some rights of memory in this kingdom,   378
Which now to claim my vantage doth invite me.   379

HORATIO
Of that I shall have also cause to speak,
And from his mouth whose voice will draw on more.   381
But let this same be presently performed,   382
Even while men's minds are wild, lest more mischance
On plots and errors happen.   384

FORTINBRAS   Let four captains
Bear Hamlet like a soldier to the stage,
For he was likely, had he been put on,   386
To have proved most royal ; and for his passage   387
The soldiers' music and the rites of war
Speak loudly for him.
Take up the bodies. Such a sight as this
Becomes the field, but here shows much amiss.
Go, bid the soldiers shoot.

> *Exeunt [marching ; after the which*
> *a peal of ordinance are shot off].*

371 *judgments* retributions; *casual* not humanly planned (reinforcing *accidental*) 372 *put on* instigated 378 *of memory* traditional and kept in mind 379 *vantage* advantageous opportunity 381 *more* i.e. more voices, or votes, for the kingship 382 *presently* immediately 384 *On* on the basis of 386 *put on* set to perform in office 387 *passage* death

APPENDIX:
DEPARTURES FROM THE TEXT
OF THE 1604–05 QUARTO

Except for a few corrections of obvious typographical errors, all departures from the text of the 1604–05 quarto (Q2) are listed below, with the adopted reading in italics followed by the rejected Q2 reading in roman. The great majority of the adopted readings are from the 1623 folio (F) and are so designated. When the adopted reading appears also in the "bad" quarto of 1603 (Q1), the fact is indicated. When the adopted reading does not occur in Q1 or F, the name of the first to make the emendation is given in most cases; otherwise (usually when the emendation is of an obvious or minor defect) the abbreviation "Eds" for "editors" is used. Quartos other than Q1 and Q2 are occasionally cited, but only when the adopted reading does not occur in F. (Actually Q4, although not regarded as of substantive value, contains a considerable number of the readings that have been adopted from F.)

I, i, 16 *soldier* (Q1, F) souldiers   33 *two nights have* (F) haue two nights   44 *harrows* (F) horrowes   61 *th' ambitious* (F) the ambitious   63 *sledded* (F) sleaded   *Polacks* (Malone) Pollax   68 *my* (Q1, F) mine   73 *why* (Q1, F) with   *cast* (F) cost   87 *heraldry* (Q1, F) heraldy   88 *those* (Q1, F) these   91 *returned* (F) returne   94 *designed* (Pope) desseigne   108 *e'en so* (Eds) enso   121 *feared* (Collier) feare   127 s.d. *He* (Q '76) It (Q2) s.d. omitted (F)   138 *you* (Q1, F) your   140 *at* (F) omitted   164 *hallowed* (F) hallowèd   175 *conveniently* (Q1, F) conuenient
I, ii, s.d. *Councillors,* (Eds) Counsaile: as   16 *all,* (Johnson) all   58 *He hath* (Q1, Q4) Hath   67 *so* (F) so much   77 *good* (F) coold   82 *shapes* (Q4) chapes (Q2) shewes (F)   85 *passeth* (F) passes   96 *a* (F) or   129 *sullied* (anon.) sallied   132 *self* (F) seale   133 *weary* (F) wary   137 *to this* (F) thus   143 *would* (Q1, F) should   148 *followed* (Rowe) followèd   149 *even she* (F) omitted   175 *to*

172

drink deep (Q1, F) for to drinke   178 *see* (Q1, F) omitted   179
followed (Eds) followèd   199 *encountered* (Eds) incountred
209 *Where, as* (Q1) Whereas   *delivered* (Q1, F) deliuerèd   213
watched (F) watch   224 *Indeed, indeed* (Q1, F) Indeede   237
Very like, very like (Q1, F) Very like   257 *Foul* (Q1, F) fonde

I, iii, 1 *embarked* (F) inbarckt   3 *convoy is* (F) conuay, in   12 *bulk*
(F) bulkes   32 *unmastered* (Eds) vnmastred   49 *like* (F) omitted
51 *recks* (Pope) reakes   68 *thine* (F) thy   74 *Are* (F) Or   75 *be*
(F) boy   76 *loan* (F) loue   83 *invites* (F) inuests   109 *Running*
(Collier) Wrong   125 *tether* (F) tider   129 *implorators* (F) im-
ploratotors   130 *bawds* (Theobald) bonds   131 *beguile* (F)
beguide

I, iv, 2 *a* (F) omitted   9 *swaggering* (Q1, F) swaggring   17 *revel*
(Q4) reueale (Q2) ll. 17–38 omitted (F)   18 *taxed* (Pope) taxèd
27 *the* (Pope) their   33 *Their* (Theobald) His   36 *evil* (Keight-
ley conjecture, withdrawn) eale   63 *will I* (Q1, F) I will   69 *lord*
(Q1, F) omitted   87 *imagination* (Q1, F) imagion

I, v, 20 *fretful* (Q1, F) fearefull   43 *wit* (Pope) wits   47 *a* (F)
omitted   53 *moved* (Eds) moouèd   55 *lust* (Q1, F) but   56 *sate*
(Q1, F) sort   62 *cursed* (Eds) cursèd   64 *leperous* (F) leaprous
68 *posset* (F) possesse   77 *Unhouseled* (Theobald) Vnhuzled
(Q2) Vnhouzzled (F)   95 *stiffly* (F) swiftly   96 *while* (F) whiles
116 *bird* (F) and   122 *my lord* (Q1, F) omitted   129 *desires* (Q1, F)
desire   132 *Look you, I'll* (F) I will   170 *some'er* (Eds) so mere

II, i, s.d. *man* (Eds) man or two   3 *marvellous* (Q4) meruiles (Q2)
maruels (F)   28 *no* (F) omitted   38 *warrant* (F) wit   39 *sullies*
(Q4) sallies (Q2) sulleyes (F)   40 *i' th'* (F) with   52–53 *at 'friend
. . . gentleman'* (F) omitted   56 *t'other* (Q1, F) th' other   58
gaming, (F) gaming   *o'ertook* (F) or tooke   63 *takes* (F) take
79 *fouled* (F) foulèd   80 *Ungartered* (Eds) Vngartred   105
passion (F) passions

II, ii, 20 *are* (F) is   43 *Assure you,* (F) I assure   57 *o'erhasty* (F)
hastie   76 *shown* (Q1, F) shone   81 *considered* (F) considerèd
90 *since* (F) omitted   97 *he is* (F) hee's   108 s.d. *letter* (placed
here as in F; at line 116 in Q2)   112 *Thus:* (Malone, from Jen-
nens substantially) thus   126 *above* (F) about   137 *winking* (F)
working   143 *his* (F) her   146 *repelled* (Eds) rèpell'd   148 *watch*
(F) wath   149 *a* (F) omitted   151 *'tis* (F) omitted   165 *fallen*
(Eds) falne   189 *far gone, far gone* (F) farre gone   190 *suffered*
(Eds) suffred   201 *you* (F) omitted   202 *should be* (F) shall grow
208 *sanity* (F) sancity   209–10 *and . . . him* (F) omitted   211

honorable (F) omitted   *most humbly* (F) omitted   213 *sir* (F) omitted   214 *will* (F) will not   222 *excellent* (F) extent   223 *ye* (F) you   225 *over-* (F) euer   226 *cap* (F) lap   234 *that* (F) omitted   269 *even* (F) euer   275 *Why, anything – but* (F) Anything but   300 *a piece* (F) peece   301 *moving how* (F) moouing, how   302 *admirable,* (F) admirable   *action* (F) action,   *angel,* (F) Angell   *apprehension* (Eds) apprehension,   305 *woman* (QI, F) women   315 *of* (F) on   318–19 *the clown . . . sere* (F) omitted   320 *blank* (QI, F) black   356 *mows* (QI, F) mouths   364 *lest my* (F) let me   389–90 *tragical-historical . . . -pastoral* (F) omitted   395 *treasure* (Walker) a treasure   415 *By'r* (F) by   419 *e'en to't* (Rowe) ento't (Q2) e'ne to't (F)   *French falconers* (QI, F) friendly Fankners   432 *affectation* (F) affection   434 *tale* (QI, F) talke   435 *where* (QI, F) when   442 *the* (QI, F) th'   462 *Then . . . Ilium* (F) omitted   469 *And* (F) omitted   483 *fellies* (Eds) follies   492 *Mobled . . . good* (F2) omitted   502 *husband's* (QI, F) husband   507 *whe'r* (Capell) where   526 *ha't* (F) hate   527 *dozen* (QI, F) dosen lines   538 *his* (F) the   540 *and* (F) an   543 *to Hecuba* (QI, F) to her   545 *the cue* (F) that   564 *ha'* (Eds) a   567 *O, vengeance!* (F) omitted   569 *father* (QI, Q4) omitted (Q2, F)   *murdered* (Eds) murtherèd   573 *About,* (Theobald) About   585 *devil . . . devil* (F) deale . . . deale

III, i, 1 *And* (F) An   28 *too* (F) two   32 *lawful espials* (F) omitted   33 *Will* (F) Wee'le   46 *loneliness* (F) lowlines   55 *Let's* (F) omitted   79 *bourn* (Capell) borne (Q2) bourne (Pope)   83 *of us all* (QI, F) omitted   85 *sicklied* (F) sickled   90 *remembered* (Eds) remembred   92 *well, well, well* (F) well   99 *the* (F) these   107 *your honesty* (F) you   121 *to* (F) omitted   121, 130, 137, 140, 149 *nunnery* (QI, F) Nunry   129 *all* (QI, F) omitted   137 *Go* (QI, F) omitted   141 *O* (F) omitted   142 *too* (F) omitted   144 *you amble* (QI, F) & amble   *lisp* (F) list   145–46 *your ignorance* (F) ignorance   147 *more* (F) mo   152 *expectancy* (F) expectation   156 *music* (F) musickt (Q2)   157 *that* (F) what   159 *feature* (F) stature   161 *see!* (F) see. Exit   188 *unwatched* (F) vnmatcht

III, ii, 9 *tatters* (F) totters   10 *split* (QI, F) spleet   18 *overdone* (F) ore-doone   21 *own* (F) omitted   24 *make* (F) makes   25 *the which* (F) which   28 *praise* (F) praysd   35 *sir* (F) omitted   49 *ho* (F) howe   86 *detecting* (F) detected   94 *now.* (Johnson) now   110 *I mean . . . lord* (these two lines are present in F, omitted in Q2)   123 *devil* (F) deule   129 s.d. *sound* (Q4) sounds   DUMB

SHOW (ll. 8, 10) *poisoner* (F) poysner   131 *is* (Q1, F) omitted
miching (Q1, F) munching   136 *counsel* (Q1, F) omitted   138
you'll (Q1, F) you will   147 *orbèd* (F) orb'd the   148 *borrowed*
(Capell) borrowèd   155 *your* (F) our   160 *In neither* (F) Eyther
none, in neither   161 *love* (F) Lord   182 *like* (F) the   191 *joys*
(F) ioy   211 *An* (Theobald) And   215 *once a* (Q1, F) once I be a
be (Q1, F) be a   220 s.d. *Exit* (Q1, F) Exeunt   232 *o'* (Q1, F) of
240 *my* (F) mine   242 *must take* (Q1) mistake   246 *Confederate*
(Q1, F) Considerat   248 *infected* (Q1, Q4) inuected   256 (this
line is present in F, omitted in Q2)   266 *two* (F) omitted   268
sir (F) omitted   274 *peacock* (Pope) paiock (Q2) pecock (Q '95)
279 *poisoning* (F) poysning   289 *distempered* (F) distempred
296 *start* (F) stare   305 *of my* (F) of   330 s.d. *Player* (Eds)
Players   344 *and thumb* (F) & the vmber   353 *the top of* (F)
omitted   357 *can fret me* (Q1, F) fret me not   371–72 *Polo-*
nius. I . . . friends. (F) Leaue me friends. / I will, say so. By and by
is easily said,   374 *breathes* (F) breakes   376 *bitter business as*
the day (F) busines as the bitter day   381 *daggers* (Q1, F) dagger

III, iii, 17 *'tis* (Dyce ii) it is   19 *huge* (F) hough   22 *ruin* (F) raine
23 *with* (F) omitted   25 *upon* (F) about   50 *pardoned* (F) pardon
58 *shove* (F) showe   69 *engaged* (F) ingagèd   73 *pat* (F) but   75
revenged (F) reuendge   79 *hire and salary* (F) base and silly   84
revenged (F) reuendgèd   89 *drunk* (F) drunke,

III, iv, 5 *with him* (F) omitted   7 *warrant* (F) wait   21 *inmost* (F)
most   23, 24 *ho* (Q1, F) how   39 *is* (F) be   50 *And* (Eds) Ore
54 *Hamlet* (placed as in F; comes one line earlier in Q2)   60
heaven-kissing (F) heaue, a kissing   65 *mildewed* (F) mildewèd
80 *sans* (Eds) sance   89 *panders* (F) pardons   90 *mine* (F) my
very   *very* (F) omitted (Q2)   91 *grainèd* (F) greeued   92 *not*
leave (F) leaue there   94 *Stewed* (F) Stewèd   96 *mine* (F) my
98 *tithe* (F) kyth   122 *hairs* (Rowe) haire   136 *lived* (Eds) liuèd
140 *Ecstasy* (F) omitted   143 *uttered* (Eds) vttred   144 *I* (F)
omitted   159 *live* (F) leaue   166 *Refrain to-night* (F) to refraine
night   171 *wondrous* (Q5) wonderous (Q2) lines omitted (F)
180 *Thus* (F) This   187 *ravel* (F) rouell   216 *foolish* (F) most
foolish

IV, i, 35 *dragged* (F) dreg'd   43 *poisoned* (Eds) poysned
IV, ii, 2 (this line is present in F, omitted in Q2)   6 *Compounded* (F)
Compound   17 *ape* (F) apple   29–30 *Hide . . . after* (F) omitted
IV, iii, 6 *weighed* (F) wayed   11 *befallen* (Eds) befalne   15 *Ho*
(F) Howe   29 *King* (F) King. King.   42 *With fiery quickness* (F)

omitted 51 *and so* (F) so 67 *were ne'er begun* (F) will nere begin
IV, v, 9 *aim* (F) yawne 16 *Queen* (Blackstone) omitted 39 *grave*
(F) ground 42 *God* (F) good 57 *la*, (F) omitted 82 *their* (F)
omitted 89 *his* (F) this 96 *Queen . . . this?* (F) omitted 97 *are*
(F) is 106 *They* (F) The 119 *brows* (Q '76) browe 152 s.d.
Let her come in (as in F, given as a speech to Laertes in Q2, at
l. 153) 156 *by* (F) with 160 *an old* (Q1, F) a poore 164 *bare-
faced* (F) bare-faste 181 *O* (F) omitted *must* (Q1, F) may
186 *affliction* (F) afflictions 194 *All* (F) omitted 198 *Christian*
(F) Christians *I pray God* (F) omitted 199 *see* (F) omitted
IV, vi, 21 *good* (F) omitted 25 *bore* (F) bord 29 *He* (F) So 30
give (F) omitted
IV, vii, 6 *proceeded* (F) proceede 7 *crimeful* (F) criminall 8
safety, (F) safetie, greatnes, 11 *they're* (Q '76) tha'r (Q2) they
are (F) 14 *conjunctive* (F) concliue 20 *Would* (F) Worke 22
loud a wind (F) loued Arm'd 24 *And* (F) But *had* (F) haue 40
received (F) receiuèd 45 *your pardon* (F) you pardon 46–47
and more strange (F) omitted 55 *shall* (F) omitted 56 *diddest*
(F) didst 60 *returned* (F) returnèd 61 *checking* (F) the King
87 *my* (F) me 114 *wick* (Rowe ii) weeke 121 *spendthrift* (Q '76)
spend thrifts (Q2) ll. 113–22 omitted (F) 122 *o'* (Eds) of
124 *yourself . . . deed* (F) your selfe indeede your fathers sonne
133 *on* (F) ore 139 *that* (F) omitted 155 *ha't* (F) hate 166
hoar (F) horry 170 *cold* (F) cull-cold
V, i, 8 *se offendendo* (F) so offended 10–11 *do, and* (F) doe, 11
Argal (F) or all 41 *frame* (F) omitted 56 *last* (Q1, Q4) lasts (Q2, F)
57 *stoup* (Q1, F) soope 62 *that* (F) omitted 63 *at* (F) in 66
daintier (F) dintier 68 *clawed* (Pope) clawèd 69 *shipped* (Eds)
shippèd *intil* (F) into 80 *meant* (F) went 82 *chapless* (F)
Choples 83 *mazzard* (F) massene 84 *an* (Capell) and 86
'em (F) them 100 *his vouchers* (F) vouchers 101 *double ones
too* (F) doubles 112 *O* (F) or 113 (line is present in F, omitted
in Q2) 130 *taken* (F) tooke 133 *a* (F) omitted 134 *all* (F)
omitted 138 *the* (F) that 155 *now-a-days* (F) omitted 162
three-and-twenty (F) 23. 169 *sir – Yorick's* (Eds) sir Yoricks
172 *Let me see* (F) omitted 174 *borne* (F) bore 181 *chamber*
(Q1, F) table 195 *as thus* (Q1, F) omitted 203 *winter's* (F)
waters 216 *have* (F) been 218 *Shards* (F) omitted 234 *treble*
(F) double 236 *Deprived* (F) Depriuèd 248 *and* (F) omitted
256 *loved* (Q1, F) louèd 264 *thou* (Q1, F) omitted 272 *thus* (F)
this 274 *disclosed* (F) disclosèd 285 *shortly* (F) thirtie

V, ii, 5 *Methought* (F) my thought   6 *bilboes* (F) bilbo   17 *unseal*
(F) vnfold   27 *me* (F) now   29 *villainies* (Capell) villaines   43
as's (Eds) as sir   46 *the* (F) those   52 *Subscribed* (F) Subscribe
55 *know'st* (F) knowest   93 *Put* (F) omitted   98 *sultry* (F) sully
for (F) or   100 *sultry* (F) soultery   101 *But* (F) omitted   105
mine (F) my   109 *feelingly* (Q4) sellingly (Q2) omitted (F)
138 *his* (Q '76) this (Q2) omitted (F)   146 *hangers* (F) hanger
152 *carriages* (F) carriage   155 *might* (F) omitted   *Barbary*
(F) Barbry (Q2)   158 *impawned, as* (Eds) omitted (Q2) impon'd
as (F)   170 *an* (Capell) and   172 *redeliver* (F) deliuer   *e'en* (F)
omitted   176 *yours. He* (F) omitted   179 *comply* (F) omitted
180 *bevy* (F) breede   182 *yeasty* (F) histy   184 *fanned . . . winnowed* (Warburton) prophane . . . trennowed   198 *this wager* (F)
omitted   201 *But* (F) omitted   204 *gaingiving* (F) gamgiuing
209 *now* (F) omitted   222 *wronged* (F) wrongèd   227 *wronged*
(F) wrongèd   229 (this line is present in F, omitted in Q2)   239
keep (F) omitted   *till* (F) all   243 *Come on* (F) omitted   252
bettered (F) better   261 *union* (F) Vnice   275 *A touch, a touch*
(F) omitted   281 *poisoned* (F) poysned   286 *but* (F) doe but
288 *afeard* (F) sure   292 *ho* (F) howe   299 *poisoned* (F) poysned
300 *Ho* (Q4) how (Q2, F)   302 *Hamlet. Hamlet* (F) Hamlet   305
thy (Q1, F) my   308 *poisoned* (F) poysned   314 *murd'rous* (F)
omitted   315 *thy* (Q1, F) the   *union* (Q1, F) Onixe   316 *served*
(F) seruèd   332 *ha't* (Capell) hate   334 *live* (F) I leaue   338
(all quartos and folios give a s.d. here: Enter Osrick)   340 *the*
(Eds) th'   347 s.d. *Dies* (Q1, F) omitted   366 *arrived* (Eds)
arriuèd   368 *th'* (F) omitted   372 *forced* (F) for no   381 *on* (F)
no   387 *proved* (Q1, F) proouèd   388 *rites* (F) right

SUPPLEMENTARY NOTES

I, i, 117 *As*   Something is obviously wrong with the transition of
thought. The conjecture that some preceding matter has been
left out of the text is perhaps as good as any.

I, ii, 129 *sullied*   Use of this emendation of the 'sallied' of the
1604–05 quarto instead of the widely accepted 'solid' of the
1623 folio is strongly recommended by : (1) the implications of
the interestingly corrupt 'too much grieu'd and sallied flesh' of
the 1603 quarto, into which the intrusive participle 'grieu'd'
cannot be thought to have come at the call of an original 'solid'

standing in the place of 'sallied'; (2) the example of the 'sallies' in a later passage of the 1604–05 quarto (II, i, 39), which in its context is most certainly to be taken as 'sullies' and which in the folio appears as 'sulleyes.'

I, iv, 37 *Doth . . . doubt* This difficult and often altered line is here printed without emendation. In the famous crux of which it is a key part the intent of what Hamlet is saying had perhaps best be taken as a close rewording of what he has just been saying; he may be taken to say that the dram of evil imparts a doubtful quality to all the noble human substance, to his (its) own scandal, i.e. to the detriment of the nobility itself because of the general censure that he has mentioned before in developing at involved length what he offers here with the emphasis of brevity.

III, iv, 162 *all sense doth eat* absorbs and lives upon all human sense, not only that made up of the bodily faculties but also the contrasting 'inward' sense made up of the faculties of the mind and soul – all sense, whether low or high and whether bad or good in use (looking forward to completion of the image of custom as a monster of double form, part devil and part angel; see the *Oxford English Dictionary* under 'Sense,' I, 3 and 7). The crux of which these words make a part has also produced frequent emendation. See the note following.

III, iv, 163 *Of habits devil* being a devil in, or in respect of, habits (with a play on 'habits,' as meaning both settled practices and garments, which by looking forward to 'actions fair and good' and to 'frock or livery' is subtly involved in the opposition and monstrous combination within the passage of devil and angel, and which contributes to an essential poetic image that tends to be destroyed by a finding of need to emend the phrase, especially when 'devil' is changed to 'evil'; see the *Oxford English Dictionary* under 'Of,' XI, 37, for a showing of the use of the preposition in the sense here given, as in the example, dated 1535, 'he yᵗ is a blabbe of his tonge').

III, iv, 170 *And . . . out* This line is usually taken to suffer from an omission after 'either' of some such word as 'master,' 'curb,' or 'quell.'

IV, i, 40 *And . . . done* It would seem that after this fragmentary line there is an omission. Capell's insertion of 'So, haply, slander,' a purely conjectural completion of the line, has often been accepted as providing desired clarification of thought.

FOR THE BEST IN PAPERBACKS, LOOK FOR THE

In every corner of the world, on every subject under the sun, Penguin represents quality and variety—the very best in publishing today.

For complete information about books available from Penguin—including Pelicans, Puffins, Peregrines, and Penguin Classics—and how to order them, write to us at the appropriate address below. Please note that for copyright reasons the selection of books varies from country to country.

In the United Kingdom: For a complete list of books available from Penguin in the U.K., please write to *Dept E.P., Penguin Books Ltd, Harmondsworth, Middlesex, UB7 0DA.*

In the United States: For a complete list of books available from Penguin in the U.S., please write to *Consumer Sales, Penguin USA, P.O. Box 999— Dept. 17109, Bergenfield, New Jersey 07621-0120.* VISA and MasterCard holders call 1-800-253-6476 to order all Penguin titles.

In Canada: For a complete list of books available from Penguin in Canada, please write to *Penguin Books Canada Ltd, 10 Alcorn Avenue, Suite 300, Toronto, Ontario, Canada M4V 3B2.*

In Australia: For a complete list of books available from Penguin in Australia, please write to the *Marketing Department, Penguin Books Ltd, P.O. Box 257, Ringwood, Victoria 3134.*

In New Zealand: For a complete list of books available from Penguin in New Zealand, please write to the *Marketing Department, Penguin Books (NZ) Ltd, Private Bag, Takapuna, Auckland 9.*

In India: For a complete list of books available from Penguin, please write to *Penguin Overseas Ltd, 706 Eros Apartments, 56 Nehru Place, New Delhi. 110019.*

In Holland: For a complete list of books available from Penguin in Holland, please write to *Penguin Books Nederland B.V., Postbus 195, NL-1380AD Weesp, Netherlands.*

In Germany: For a complete list of books available from Penguin, please write to *Penguin Books Ltd, Friedrichstrasse 10-12, D-6000 Frankfurt Main 1, Federal Republic of Germany.*

In Spain: For a complete list of books available from Penguin in Spain, please write to *Longman, Penguin España, Calle San Nicolas 15, E-28013 Madrid, Spain.*

In Japan: For a complete list of books available from Penguin in Japan, please write to *Longman Penguin Japan Co Ltd, Yamaguchi Building, 2-12-9 Kanda Jimbocho, Chiyoda-Ku, Tokyo 101, Japan.*

The Pelican Shakespeare

_____	0-14-071430-8	**All's Well That Ends Well** Barish (ed.)
_____	0-14-071420-0	**Antony and Cleopatra** Mack (ed.)
_____	0-14-071417-0	**As You Like It** Sargent (ed.)
_____	0-14-071432-4	**The Comedy of Errors** Jorgensen (ed.)
_____	0-14-071402-2	**Coriolanus** Levin (ed.)
_____	0-14-071428-6	**Cymbeline** Heilman (ed.)
_____	0-14-071405-7	**Hamlet** Farnham (ed.)
_____	0-14-071407-3	**Henry IV, Part I** Shaaber (ed.)
_____	0-14-071408-1	**Henry IV, Part II** Chester (ed.)
_____	0-14-071409-X	**Henry V** Harbage (ed.)
_____	0-14-071434-0	**Henry VI (Revised Edition), Part I** Bevington (ed.)
_____	0-14-071435-9	**Henry VI (Revised Edition), Parts II and III** Bevington (ed.) Turner (ed.)
_____	0-14-071436-7	**Henry VIII** Hoeniger (ed.)
_____	0-14-071422-7	**Julius Caesar** Johnson (ed.)
_____	0-14-071426-X	**King John** Ribner (ed.)
_____	0-14-071414-6	**King Lear** Harbage (ed.)
_____	0-14-071427-8	**Love's Labor's Lost** Harbage (ed.)
_____	0-14-071401-4	**Macbeth** Harbage (ed.)
_____	0-14-071403-0	**Measure for Measure** Bald (ed.)
_____	0-14-071421-9	**The Merchant of Venice** Stirling (ed.)
_____	0-14-071424-3	**The Merry Wives of Windsor** Bowers (ed.)

FOR THE BEST IN PAPERBACKS, LOOK FOR THE

_____ 0-14-071418-9 **A Midsummer Night's Dream** Doral (ed.)

_____ 0-14-071412-X **Much Ado About Nothing** Bennett (ed.)

_____ 0-14-071437-5 **The Narrative Poems** Shakespeare

_____ 0-14-071410-3 **Othello** Bentley (ed.)

_____ 0-14-071438-3 **Pericles** McManaway (ed.)

_____ 0-14-071406-5 **Richard II** Black (ed.)

_____ 0-14-071416-2 **Richard III** Evans (ed.)

_____ 0-14-071419-7 **Romeo and Juliet** Hankins (ed.)

_____ 0-14-071423-5 **Sonnets** Shakespeare

_____ 0-14-071425-1 **The Taming of the Shrew** Hosley (ed.)

_____ 0-14-071415-4 **The Tempest** Frye (ed.)

_____ 0-14-071429-4 **Timon of Athens** Hinman (ed.)

_____ 0-14-071433-2 **Titus Andronicus** Cross (ed.)

_____ 0-14-071413-8 **Troilus and Cressida** Whitaker (ed.)

_____ 0-14-071411-1 **Twelfth Night** Prouty (ed.)

_____ 0-14-071431-6 **The Two Gentlemen of Verona (Revised Edition)** Jackson (ed.)

_____ 0-14-071404-9 **The Winter's Tale** Maxwell (ed.)

The Penguin Shakespeare

_____ 0-14-070720-4 **All's Well That Ends Well** Everett (ed.)

_____ 0-14-070731-X **Antony and Cleopatra** Jones (ed.)

_____ 0-14-070714-X **As You Like It** Oliver (ed.)

_____ 0-14-070725-5 **The Comedy of Errors** Wells (ed.)

_____ 0-14-070703-4 **Coriolanus** Hibbard (ed.)

_____ 0-14-070734-4 **Hamlet** Spencer (ed.)

_____ 0-14-070718-2 **Henry IV, Part I** Davison (ed.)

_____ 0-14-070728-X **Henry IV, Part II** Davison (ed.)

_____ 0-14-070708-5 **Henry V** Humphreys (ed.)

_____ 0-14-070735-2 **Henry VI, Part I** Sanders (ed.)

_____ 0-14-070736-0 **Henry VI, Part II** Sanders (ed.)

_____ 0-14-070737-9 **Henry VI, Part III** Sanders (ed.)

_____ 0-14-070722-0 **Henry VIII** Humphreys (ed.)

_____ 0-14-070704-2 **Julius Caesar** Sanders (ed.)

_____	0-14-070727-1	**King John** Smallwood (ed.)
_____	0-14-070724-7	**King Lear** Hunter (ed.)
_____	0-14-070738-7	**Love's Labour's Lost** Kerrigan (ed.)
_____	0-14-070705-0	**Macbeth** Hunter (ed.)
_____	0-14-070715-8	**Measure for Measure** Nosworthy (ed.)
_____	0-14-070706-9	**The Merchant of Venice** Merchant (ed.)
_____	0-14-070726-3	**The Merry Wives of Windsor** Hibbard (ed.)
_____	0-14-070702-6	**A Midsummer Night's Dream** Wells (ed.)
_____	0-14-070709-3	**Much Ado About Nothing** Foakes (ed.)
_____	0-14-070707-7	**Othello** Muir (ed.)
_____	0-14-070729-8	**Pericles** Edwards (ed.)
_____	0-14-070723-9	**The Rape of Lucrece** Lever (ed.)
_____	0-14-070719-0	**Richard II** Wells (ed.)
_____	0-14-070712-3	**Richard III** Honigmann (ed.)
_____	0-14-070701-8	**Romeo and Juliet** Spencer (ed.)
_____	0-14-070732-8	**Sonnets and A Lover's Complaint** Shakespeare
_____	0-14-070710-7	**The Taming of the Shrew** Hibbard (ed.)
_____	0-14-070713-1	**The Tempest** Righter (ed.)
_____	0-14-070721-2	**Timon of Athens** Hibbard (ed.)
_____	0-14-070741-7	**Troilus and Cressida** Foakes (ed.)

FOR THE BEST IN PAPERBACKS, LOOK FOR THE